SEASIDE RUMORS

NELLIE BROOKS

Merpaper Press

Cover design by Nellie Brooks

ISBN: 978-1-958957-02-8

Contents

CHAPTER 1

September vanished like the morning fogs hugging the forested cliffs and sandy beaches of Bay Harbor, and the first day of October washed over town and trees like a wave of fiery rubies, shining gold, and glowing emeralds. The orchard behind the blue house at 12 Seasweet Lane was full of red and yellow apples as sweet and plump as the trees were old and their branches crooked.

Sisley stood among the blazing foliage in one of her grandmother Julie's flowing dresses, pondering her next move. A sea breeze—not as warm as the day before but crisp with the scent of salt and sea—tugged on her long skirt, tangling it around her ankles. Sisley loved wearing Julie's clothes; they felt like home. Julie was close to her in moments like this, when she was alone with only the rumbling sea for company.

Well, not *quite* alone.

Sisley's gaze slipped to the baby sleeping in the sling tied around her chest. Then it wandered to the ringless hand cradling Lovie.

Her mother Mela remembered Julie wearing a lapis lazuli ring that she wanted Sisley to have. They'd searched; but the ring had been lost to time or maybe the sea on that fateful day when Julie and her brother Finn did not return from their boating trip. It stung to let go of the only piece of jewelry Julie had owned, but in the big picture it didn't matter.

Wiping a blond strand of hair from her face, Sisley returned to her business, wondering whether she should pick one more apple. It was sitting right there on the branch in front of her, tempting her. But her basket was full to the brim, already weighing twice as much as the baby. And even though she was only a month old, Lovie was as heavy as one of the orange Halloween pumpkins growing near the sun-drenched stone wall.

"Sunny said to bring the rest of the apples, but this is all I can carry," she decided. Lovie couldn't understand, but Sisley always talked to her as if she could. Who knew when exactly words started to make sense to a baby?

She hitched Lovie higher so she could press a kiss on the soft hair and inhale the sweet baby scent. Then she went back to the house, passing the barn where her mother kept the beekeeping equipment, and the garden, where blooming asters and mums had replaced the nodding heads of lavender and hydrangeas. A pair of sliding glass doors led into the living room, and then it was only a few steps to the kitchen.

Her grandaunt Sunny was sitting at the small table, listening to the radio and peeling apples. The kitchen was warm and bright and sunflower-yellow because Julie had painted the cabinets many years ago. Despite the early hour, the scents of cinnamon and nutmeg and boiling cream filled the air. Sisley set down her basket and stretched out her back. It creaked and cracked. "This is all I could pick," Sisley said and laughed at how feeble pregnancy had left her.

Sunny peered over the frame of her half-glasses at the basket. "I think I will make one more batch today, and then we have enough pies to get through the winter." She nodded at three pies with artfully woven lattices cooling on the counter. "Maybe Peter will pick the rest later and we'll use them for winter apples. Or applesauce. You can never have enough applesauce." Sunny busily put down her knife and stood.

"Look at you," Sisley said. "Your hip is in better shape than mine."

Sunny walked over to her without a limp. Her hip replacement had worked out better than expected, and she was ecstatic to walk again. The site was still a little swollen and sore at the end of the day, but she never complained. Sisley only knew about it because Mom kept a close eye on the healing wound.

"That surgery was the best thing I ever did in my life," Sunny said contently. "Apart from all the other best things that happened to me. Like getting to spend time with this little cutie." She tickled Lovie, who had woken up and was peeking out of the sling. "Are you about ready to give your back a break? I'll take her if you'll share."

"Yes. Thank you." Sisley loosened the sling and lifted the baby out, handing her over.

"Who's a baby?" Sunny cooed and snuggled Lovie. The baby had just started to lift her head and used the new skill to stare at Sunny with fascination. "Yes—you are!" Sunny answered herself. "You are the baby."

Sisley smiled and untied the empty sling. It was intricately woven silk in rich jewel colors, a present from her sister Kimmie. She set it on a kitchen chair where it was safe from catching stains. The entire table was taken up with boards and bowls and apple peel and mason jars of honey and forgotten, half-full mugs of tea and cider. All week people had drifted in and out of the kitchen, pitching in with the apple and the honey harvest.

"Maybe *you* should take a break," Sisley suggested. "You've been cooking and baking nonstop. You're supposed to take it easy on the new hip."

"Ah, fiddlesticks. This is nothing compared to the pain I was in before. I made jam before the sun was up," Sunny declared proudly. "The blackberries are out of control this year and so are the elderberries. I thought the blackbirds would get to them before I did, but there's plenty to go around. In fact, I think I'll go pick more."

"If you're sure." Sisley pointed at the table, crowded with apple pie paraphernalia. "I'd offer to help, but I finally talked Mom into letting me clean out the attic."

Sisley also felt almost fully healed after delivering her baby, and the packed attic was calling to her. Her fingers itched with the desire to clean it out, so it wasn't a health or fire hazard up there.

"You're not yet supposed to do heavy lifting." Sunny squinted at her.

"Bennett will help with that."

"Ah, Bennett's helping. I see." The corner of Sunny's mouth twitched, and then she made a shooing motion with her hand. "Go ahead, go ahead. I don't need your help. I'm as sprightly as a—sprite. Whatever that is."

Sisley reached to take Lovie back, but Sunny swiveled protectively. "I can take her."

"You don't want to take her berry picking," Sisley warned. The baby was quiet but agile and given to suddenly throwing herself backward like a wayward whale. "Besides. You must be tired despite all your sprightliness."

"I was just going to have a coffee break," Sunny said, clearly making it up on the spot. "The berries can use another day of sunshine."

"Fine." When it came to babysitters, Sisley was a millionaire. She didn't have money, but she rarely had to ask when she needed a hand. In fact, often enough she felt like she had to get in line herself to snag a turn with her daughter, but after worrying for nine months that she and Lovie would have to go it alone, she was grateful.

The doorbell rang.

"That'll be Bennett," Sisley said. She shook her hair back and smoothed her dress where the sling had crumpled it. "How do I look?"

"Good enough for Bennett, I'm sure." Sunny sounded stern, but she couldn't help but smile. "You're the spitting image of your grandmother. Blond and skinny as a twig. You've even got her biscuit tan. No wonder your mom and I keep thinking we're seeing Julie. It's like having a living ghost in the house."

Sisley had seen the few pictures the family had of Julie. She saw differences in the shape of the nose and the turn of the chin, but she also saw the striking resemblance. "I wish I could have met her," she said wistfully. "It's a bummer to look like someone you and Mom loved so much and never get to meet them."

"I wish you could have met her too, honey. She'd have been over the moon to have a granddaughter like you. You're both soft and sweet—and somewhat secretive." She raised her eyebrows significantly at Lovie.

By the time Sisley had finally admitted her pregnancy to the family, Lovie had been baked to perfection. Julie, too, had been a single mother, though she'd never revealed who the father was.

Sisley laughed but goosebumps trickled down her arms. "I'm not *secretive*; I was scared and out of touch. I'm the least secretive person in the world." The words tumbled out too hastily, and she cleared her throat.

She'd never told anyone about the strange things she'd experienced in Bay Harbor.

A moment from last month flashed through Sisley's mind. She'd been painting a watercolor in the field by the sea. The rest of the family had been busy making honey in the barn, so she'd been on her own—until she heard a voice behind her. It distinctly said *beautiful.*

Only that one word.

Beautiful.

At first, Sisley had thought the voice had come from the baby monitor and that somebody was talking to Lovie, who was napping in her crib in the nursery. But when she hurried inside to check, there was nobody there.

If it had been any other word, Sisley might have been worried about the state of her mind. But who heard the word *beautiful* when they went crazy?

Nobody.

Right?

The bell rang again.

"Oops!" Sisley swirled and ran to yank open the front door. "Sorry!" She beamed at Bennett. "No need to ring! It's always open!"

Bennett Cobb was a detective in Sandville, the nearest town with a police department big enough to employ detectives. He was also tall and dark and handsome, and the son of Mom's best friend, Amelie. Amelie's love of cooking matched Sunny's, and Bennett held a massive covered aluminum tray in his hands. He held it up to show why he hadn't opened the door himself.

"I thought you weren't going to let me in," he said good-humoredly. "What with me bringing baked ziti and everything."

"I'm so sorry. I should've known your mom would make you bring food for twelve." Sisley stepped aside so he could come in. She held her breath as he passed so she wouldn't breathe in his scent. The way he smelled deliciously of books and tea and cozy afternoons in the twilight was disconcerting. She already had a crush a mile wide on him and was determined to root it out as efficiently as the poison ivy that ruined the field behind the orchard.

Her last relationship had taught her to stay away from men, especially the ones that were too good to be true, the ones she crushed on. She'd been incredibly, undeservedly lucky to fall on her feet after her last attempt in the dating department; instead of love, she'd invited abuse into her life. She'd promised herself and her daughter that it would never happen again. Never.

"Why are you holding your breath?" Bennett lifted the covered tray and sniffed. "Is it the sauce? I told Mom it was too much garlic."

"No, no, it smells fantastic." Sisley closed the door on the bright afternoon and exhaled. "I have the hiccups," she lied and led the way into the kitchen. "I heard holding your breath helps."

She found herself lying to Bennett more and more often. She couldn't go have ice cream at the harbor because Lovie had an upset tummy. She had to take a raincheck on the morning beach walk because she'd barely gotten any sleep and was bone-tired.

Sisley didn't like lying to Bennett. Now that her sister wasn't in town anymore, he and her house mate Johanna were practically her best friends in the world.

But she couldn't stop making up excuses. Because Bennett didn't stop asking. He simply didn't get the message. It made hiding her crush even more difficult, and the lies made her hate herself.

Sisley knew all about men making her hate herself. For some time, the only solution she could come up with was to draw a line.

But it was hard to draw that line. Sisley had no idea how to go about it without hurting her friend. If she knew what to say, she'd have done it already.

While Bennett kissed Sunny's cheek and tickled Lovie's belly like a besotted uncle, Sisley wondered whether one of these days, she'd simply have to tell him.

Only she had one of those Bay Harbor feelings squirming in her chest like a sea serpent about to burst the surface. If she told Bennett she wasn't in love with him, he wouldn't want to stay friends.

Attic and ziti aside—Sisley still very much wanted to be his friend.

Chapter 2

"After you." Bennett had lowered the ladder to the attic and gestured Sisley should go first. "I'll catch you if you fall." He looked dead-serious.

"Oh. Uh. You go first." Bennett was a gentleman, but Sisley didn't want her butt right in front of his face. "I don't want to poke my head up there and get swatted by the attic ghost," she lied. "You do it."

"All right." Bennett's eyes crinkled, and he climbed the ladder without hesitation. When he disappeared from sight, Sisley went too, feeling ashamed for her pettiness. It was too easy to boss Bennett around. He was too friendly. If her ex had said for her to hop up the ladder, she'd have done it without a peep.

"Are you okay?" Bennett held out a hand, and Sisley grabbed it. He pulled her up. The force of her momentum made her bump into his chest.

Hastily, she stepped back, smiling to make it better. "I'm fine. I'm... I've never been up here. Wow."

All around them, boxes and chests and baskets and cartons were tumbled together, decorated with a thick layer of dust. A ray of light fell through an opening in the siding that was too small to be a proper window. Motes swam in the stifling air, and the scent of molded books and drying glue, aged fabric, and disintegrating carton filled the air.

Bennett waved a hand in front of his face even though there was no fresh air to replace the old. Sisley coughed and pulled two pairs of rubber gloves from the voluminous pockets of Julie's dress. "Here, take these." Her voice was scratchy with dust. "The sooner we get out of here and back downstairs, the better."

Bennett took her gloves and looked at them. "These are well too small for my hands," he said mildly and handed them back. "Luckily, I always carry my own." He pulled a pair from the back pocket of his jeans and expertly slipped them on.

"Ah," Sisley said wisely. "Because you're a detective."

"That's right." He lifted a carton from the top of a pile. "How do we do this? Do you want to have a look inside right now?"

Sisley coughed again and went deeper into the attic. "I think we just need to get everything out. What do you think?"

Instead of answering, Bennett went to the tiny opening in the siding, weaving his way around stacks and piles and towers of stuff.

"What are you doing?" Sisley called after him. She heard some clonking and banging, and suddenly, sunlight and fresh air streamed into the attic. She inhaled thankfully and stepped around the boxes covering her view. "Oh. Whoa!"

The entire siding seemed to be gone. There had been more than a window—there had been doors. Bennett stood beside them, looking out contently. "I thought so," he told her. "This is probably one of the old fishing cottages they built back in the day. The door is for hauling things in and out of the attic. There probably used to be a beam going out over the yard."

Sisley leaned forward to peek outside. "What in all the names were they hauling?" she asked. The sea glistened in the gold and silver the sun poured on the water. Far out was a small ship, a sliver of white on the shimmering blue. It was beautiful.

Reflexively, Bennett put out his hand, ready to grab her. "Not so close, Sis. There's no railing to prevent a fall, and the rain might have come through the slit in the doors here. Who knows, the floorboards might be rotten."

Sisley's thoughts flew to her baby. She took a step back. "Well, that changes everything, doesn't it?"

"Yes," he said seriously. "I do not want to see you crash through that floor."

She turned, surprised, and then she chuckled. "No, I mean having these doors changes everything. If we toss things through them, they'll just land on the grass by the patio. Much easier than carrying everything down the ladder."

"That too," said Bennett.

"I suppose we should have a look into the boxes after all. Trash can go on the grass, and maybe Peter can spare the dumpster later. But If I want to keep it for

Mom, we'll bring it down the ladder and put it in the spare room?"

"Sure. I'm here to do whatever needs doing." Bennett crossed his arms.

She smiled. "Thank you, Bennett. It's kind of you to help. Has anyone ever told you that you look exactly like a detective?"

"No," he claimed, stone-faced. "You're the first. Do I really?"

She lightly touched his arm. "Yes. I think it's the gloves." Later, when she thought back to the moment, she thought he shrank from her touch. Not much, almost imperceptibly. But not entirely.

"Well, let's start," he said and stepped around her, pulling down a wicker basket. He opened the lid. "What's this? Shoes?"

"Oh yes, they are! Look! Wedges!" Sisley pulled out a pair of straw wedges that looked straight from the seventies. "These are vintage! And in good shape." She turned them in the light. They weren't expensive shoes by any means, and she had no idea why Julie would've put them in the attic, but she liked them anyway.

"Do they fit you?" Bennett sounded amused.

"Are you laughing at me?" Sisley held the shoe to the sole of her tennis shoes. "Yes, they'd fit. I like it!"

"I'm laughing at how slow this will go," Bennett remarked, taking the wedge from her hands and putting it back in the basket. "Let's make a pile with boxes to save." He pushed the basket into a corner. "Right. Next."

Sisley pulled a carton closer. She'd been cleared by her doctor, but her body was not entirely where it'd been before giving birth, and she was still weary of too much lifting. "What's this?" She looked up and grinned. "It's a bit like Christmas, isn't it?"

"A bit," Bennett said dryly and pulled a sock from the box. "Old clothes. Anything good?"

"No." Sisley rooted through a pile of dusty clothes. "If she had nice things in here, they're all downstairs already."

"Dump." Bennett pushed the box near the opening. "Let's wait for Peter's dumpster before we toss it down. We don't want a bunch of socks and petticoats on the lawn."

Sisley nodded. So he had seen the petticoats. "Not much escapes your notice."

"It's my job. Next." He put another box in front of her.

"It's a china set, I think. I...don't like it." The set had something old-fashioned to it. Older than the fun vintage vibe of the wedges. But instead of thinking of the set as an antique, it made Sisley think of stuffy Sunday teas where mother was watching hawkeyed that nothing happened to the good china. "Ugh," she said, lifting one of the saucers. "I *really* don't like it."

"I kind of do," Bennett said, sounding surprised. "What's that? Little roses?"

"Do you want it?"

He shook his head. "I think you should ask your mom if she does."

"Yes." She put the saucer back and wiped her hands. "Of course. You're right. It's not mine to give away." She folded the box shut and pushed it into the pile.

Bennett tilted his head. "That's the discard pile." He pointed. "This is the one to keep."

"Right." Sisley slid the box over to the other side. "Next?"

"Next." Bennett opened another box. "This one's books."

Sisley pulled out one of them. "Oh. It smells. Phooey."

"Maybe they got moldy." Bennett took the book from her hand and turned it over. *One Hundred Years of Solitude*. "I read that." He put it with the rest and closed the box. "But if it's moldy...throw it out?"

Suddenly, Sisley's stomach cramped. "Ow!" She exhaled tightly and pressed a hand to it. Bennett was beside her, taking her arm, holding her up. "You shouldn't have... You lifted the china, didn't you?"

She leaned into him. Not because she had to, but because she wanted to. He smelled so good, and the pain in her stomach shocked her. "I only slid it over the floor." She exhaled again. "I'm okay. I think."

"Yeah? I think we should go back downstairs. It's too much too soon, Sisley. The stuff has been up here for decades. It might as well wait a couple of weeks longer."

"No," Sisley said before she could think. "It can't wait any longer. The books—definitely keep the books." The pain lessened, the cramp receded, and warm relief spread in her stomach. "Yes. Hey—I'm better already."

"Are you sure?"

She smiled up at him. He was awfully close; she could see flecks of gold in his brown eyes. "Sure about the books or the cramp?"

"Both." He looked worried.

Sisley rested her head on his shoulder. She'd wanted to do it for a long while now. Just once. Just to see how it felt. "I'm sure. Let's keep going. Let's keep the books."

They stood, Sisley's blond hair and flowy dress moving gently in the sea breeze.

She needed to lift her head, to step away. Now. Now. Now.

"Sisley," he murmured, and she could hear in his voice that she'd waited too long.

"Oh. No. No." Quickly, she stepped away and turned to look at him. She clutched her hands. "I'm sorry, Bennett."

He didn't reply, just kept looking at her with his dark eyes.

"I'm so sorry," she whispered. "I really am."

"Can we talk?"

"No." Sisley exhaled. That's what Lars had said at first—*Can we talk?* She'd learned quickly that it was dangerous to talk. It never made things better and always worse. "I just... It's not... No, Bennett. There's nothing to talk about."

Finally, he looked away. First out the window at the sea, then the sky, then at the spot above her head. His expression didn't change, but Sisley could feel the muscles and skin harden from the inside. When he spoke, his voice came from a vast, empty place. "Should we keep going?"

"You don't have to," Sisley said hastily. "I'll ask my brother to help. It's no problem."

"Morris is at the motel," Bennett said in his new empty voice. "Let's keep going. What's in this box?"

Sisley leaned to look but didn't step closer. "It's winter scarves and gloves." She felt nothing about them. "Throw it away." She leaned back.

Without commenting, Bennett shoved the box in the discard corner. "This one?"

"Trash."

And on they went. Sisley felt nothing more about Grandma Julie's things, and Bennett's monotonous voice matched her feelings.

Finally, Bennett pulled the gloves off and tossed them on the trash pile. "I have to pick up Nana," he said and checked his phone.

Sisley hated it when someone was mad at her. It was unsafe; the tension in the air was a raised hand ready to strike. And again, it was her own fault. She shouldn't have rested her head on his shoulder. She shouldn't have asked him to help. She should never even have thought of Bennett as a friend.

She was terrible with men.

The worst.

Sisley swallowed the bitter taste in her mouth and cast around for something to say that would disarm the spring-loaded atmosphere.

The words came out wooden and dry and scared. "Is your nana playing canasta with her friends?"

"That's the best-case scenario." Bennett gave a weak smile. For a moment, the tension lifted. "I wanted to tell you something," he murmured.

Sisley looked at her feet, her heart hammering. Was this the strike she'd meant to avoid?

"But now...now I think I made a mistake," Bennett said softly. "I'd better leave, Sisley."

Sisley forced herself to look up. "I hope...I hope—"

"It's all right. Don't worry." He nodded, and then he turned and climbed down the ladder, leaving Sisley alone in the attic.

CHAPTER 3

Sisley sat down on a dusty box by the window, staring out at the sea. She wanted to cry, but her eyes were so dry they hurt.

Some perverse part of her screamed for Bennett to come back, to stop leaving the house and climb back up the ladder, smiling as if nothing had happened, as if he didn't hate her now. But the rest of her knew they couldn't be friends. There was too much chemistry; almost from the moment they met, the air between them had been unhealthily magnetic.

The sea breeze flapped a strand of hair on her cheek. It felt like a soft slap from a hand, and it woke her from her misery. There was still lots to do even if she didn't shift boxes. She could peek into them and mark them for the two piles. She pulled out the marker she'd brought and rose.

She had a daughter now. She couldn't allow herself to wallow, even if she had just ruined a friendship.

For another half hour or so, Sisley numbly opened and closed boxes, designating them as needed. Not all of the things seemed to be Julie's; there were also heavy fishermen's sweaters and knitted caps, fishing gear, boxes full of baseball mitts and cleats, and dank duffle coats with broad shoulders and narrow waists. Clearly, the people who lived in the house before Julie moved in had forgotten to take their things out of the attic before selling it. When her stomach grumbled, Sisley stopped.

She turned. Many boxes were still left to check, but she was hungry and sad, and she was tired. She needed to go down and check on Lovie.

Her gaze fell on a small wicker chest in the far corner.

Before she knew what she was doing, she'd walked over and laid her hands on the rough, woven lid, opening it.

"Papers?" She picked one up. It was an essay, scrawled in a loopy child's hand. On the top, Sisley spotted Julie's name. "Her school things," she whispered and lifted out a book. "Geography." She flipped through the book, but the paper had become smelly with mildew. She closed it. A photo fluttered to the ground. It hadn't been inside the book but stuck to the back, sticky from the years in the chest.

Sisley picked it up. A man was standing on the beach in short swim trunks, kelp draped around his neck like a slippery scarf, laughing at the photographer. The photo was black-and-white, but even so, Sisley could tell the man was tan and handsome, with wavy hair and light eyes. She flipped the photo over.

Finn Sullivan, it said in faint pencil strokes.

Sisley looked back at the man. Julie's brother Finn? The one who had built the boat that had sunk, taking the unfortunate siblings with it?

She closed the chest but kept the photo. Mom would love to see it. She had no other picture of her uncle, and very few memories besides. Sisley went to shutter the window so it couldn't rain into the attic, then found her way in the dim light to the ladder and climbed down.

She washed her hands and then went into the kitchen, clutching her find. "Mom? Sunny?"

"Out here," Sunny called, and Sisley joined her on the patio. Her grandaunt was holding Lovie, who was sucking thoughtfully on her tiny fist. "I thought we'd catch a bit of sun," Sunny explained. "Did Bennett leave already?"

Sisley moistened her lip. "He had to pick up Meredith."

"Aha. Is she at the canasta again?" Sunny grinned. "What do you have there?"

Sisley showed her the photo. "That's Finn, isn't it? Mom's uncle, Julie's brother?"

"Goodness." Sunny put on the glasses that were always either dangling on a chain around her neck or, when Lovie was in Sunny's arms, tucked into her hair. "I met him only once that I can remember, and he wasn't wearing swim trunks then. Your grandmother didn't share her brother. Nor would my first husband have liked it either." She raised her eyebrows. "This man is handsome, isn't he? Can't say I recognize him."

"It was in one of Julie's boxes, with her old school things. There's a name on the back." Sisley turned the photo around and showed Sunny the scribbled marks.

Her grandaunt squinted. "Time for a new prescription. I can't read this. What does it say?"

"It says Finn Sullivan."

Sunny tugged the glasses from Lovie's grasp. "Sullivan? The family name was Palmer. Julie Palmer."

"That's right." Sisley hadn't noticed. "It was Palmer. Maybe it's a different Finn?"

"How many Finns can one girl know?" Sunny pursed her lips. "Though...my name wasn't Palmer either."

"Oh." Sisley let the photograph sink. "Another child Grandma Constance wasn't allowed to keep?"

They looked at each other until Sunny shook her head. "No way. Constance wouldn't have... She wouldn't have... Not *twice*."

"No," Sisley agreed. "From what Mom told me, Constance was in enough trouble after having you. It's too unlikely."

"Then maybe it's a different Finn after all." Sunny shrugged.

Sisley took Lovie and pressed a kiss on the chubby cheek. Lovie squealed and kicked her legs, clearly hungry and ready to have her mom take care of her.

"I'll nurse Lovie, and then I'll take her over to the Bay Harbor Motel. Mom's the only one who knows what Finn looked like. She'll be able to tell us if this is her uncle."

Sunny rose, stretching her arms. "You do that. I'll finish peeling the apples. Are you hungry?"

Sisley nodded. "Very." She hadn't noticed.

"Do you want me to heat Amelie's baked ziti while you nurse?"

Sisley's appetite was gone as quickly as it had sprung up. "Oh, I don't know. Maybe I'll eat later. Or just a sandwich."

"A sandwich if you can have Amelie's baked ziti?" Sunny studied her over the half-glasses. "And Bennett left without saying bye to Lovie? Now, why would he do that?"

Sisley hugged her daughter. "I can make the sandwich myself."

"Oh, baby girl." Sunny sighed. "Did you tell him?"

Sisley swallowed. She nodded, not trusting herself to speak.

"Okay." Sunny dropped her glasses. "I'll make you a sandwich if that's really what you want. But it'll be dry and boring. Baked pasta with ricotta and a nice juicy meat filling is much more interesting."

The double entendre made Sisley look up. "Really, Sunny? Really?"

"I'm just saying!" Sunny lifted her hands defensively. "You do you, sweet baby angel. We can't all lead interesting lives."

"All right. Fine. I'll be back in a few minutes, and then I'll take my sandwich over to the motel," Sisley said.

“Let me know what your mom says.” Sunny patted Sisley’s arm. “I’ll watch Lovie. At least you should eat your dry sandwich in peace.”

Sisley pressed a kiss on the withered cheek. “Thank you.”

She nursed and changed Lovie and hummed her asleep before putting her into her crib for an overdue nap. “I’ll see you in an hour, love bug.” She switched on the baby monitor and tiptoed out of the room, waiting outside the door until Lovie’s squawks of protest turned into sleepy snuffles and finally, soft snores.

In the kitchen, she swapped the monitor for the not-at-all dry ham sandwich her grandaunt handed her, and then she walked through the salty heat of the early afternoon to the Bay Harbor Motel.

Chapter 4

Mela ran a finger along the edge of the new table in the motel room.

When she first returned to Bay Harbor, she'd stayed in this room. It'd been clean but shabby, and it'd been only one of two rooms fit for guests.

Since then, the motel had gotten a structural and cosmetic upgrade. Each couple of tiny rooms had been merged into a suite that was comfortably large and equipped with new cottage-style furniture, cheerily framed seascapes, and mirrors to reflect daylight into every corner.

What before was dull was now bright and inviting, with large windows, potted greenery, and a spacious sea-view balcony making for a spa-like atmosphere of light and air and relaxation.

"I'm impressed," she admitted. "It looks even better than I thought it would. I know it doesn't have enough rooms to qualify, but now it feels more like a hotel instead of a motel."

"I couldn't have done in ten years what the professionals did in less than a month," Peter agreed. "Goes to show that you need the right tools for the job, doesn't it?"

Mela hummed her agreement. "Definitely." For a long time, Peter had tried to fix up the decaying motel his father had left him. It had drained his savings, but it had never been enough to attract new guests to the former beauty.

"Lucky break." Peter chuckled.

This time, an entire crew had come from Bay Port, bringing big equipment and dozens of people who knew exactly what they were doing. The remodel had taken less than two weeks, and the furnishing had been done in another. The money had come from Peter's brother Charlie, who had financed the costly renovation in return for being made business partner.

It'd been a generous offer. Peter had offered to simply take Charlie on since it'd been their father's motel. But Charlie had insisted.

Maisie opened a white cabinet. There was a glossy flatscreen TV inside. A far cry from the bulky set she'd watched the news on not so long ago. "Do you remember Sunny putting her doilies everywhere?" She closed the door again. "She even decorated her set."

"I'll never forget the dreaded doilies." Peter had housed Sunny for two years before she moved in with Mela. "By the way, I noticed she doesn't do that at your place."

"Maybe it was her way of turning a motel room into a home."

They went back out on the long balcony that ran street-side along the entire upper level and took the pretty and new stable staircase down to the reception. Mela peeked into a couple more rooms on the way, and Peter pointed out this and that improvement.

"So we have a dozen beautiful rooms, a conference room, and a dining hall." He returned to his customary spot behind the reception counter. Only now, there was a shiny new computer on it instead of the tattered ledger. "All we need are guests to fill them."

Mela went to the club chairs that had been delivered that morning and sat. They still smelled of plastic wrapping and snowy down stuffing. "Uh. Comfy."

"Charlie picked them out online."

"You were on the phone with him yesterday, weren't you? Did you talk about attracting guests?"

"We tossed some ideas around." Peter sighed. "We'll advertise. Put an ad in the local Sandpaper, and maybe the Starfish Report over in Beach Cove. They're swamped with tourists. We'll see how it goes."

"You don't seem very hopeful."

"What we really need in this business are word-of-mouth recommendations," Peter said. "One person enjoying their stay and telling their friends about it. I don't think an ad is going to convince anyone to pick us over a motel in Sandville."

"It would help if we had some tourist attractions. Sandville has golf courses and restaurants and movie theaters galore."

"And their beaches are just as good as ours," Peter added glumly. "No reason to bother driving out here."

"Our beaches are empty," Mela corrected. "That's a big plus, isn't it? Beach Cove and Sandville are so crowded in the summer it's hard to even get a good parking spot. Anyone trying to go to the beach with a toddler would cry tears of gratitude for our easy parking. Schlepping all those umbrellas and toys and ice chests along the road is nobody's idea of a fun time." She nodded sagely. She'd seen the families close to cracking as they trudged the roadside when they should've been enjoying themselves building sandcastles by the water.

"Maybe." Peter still sounded doubtful. "But you'll always need a handful of tourists to attract more. Nobody wants beaches that are *too* empty. It's spooky. Those toddlers need friends to play with."

"I'll have the kids invite their friends next summer," Mela promised. "Maybe that and whoever answers the ads will be enough of a crowd to get started."

"Please do ask the kids. We should try and get to know their friends." Peter nodded his agreement. "I want to know what everyone is up to."

Mela smiled at him; not for the first time, she wondered how she possibly deserved Peter. "I agree."

Robert, Mela's ex-husband and father of Kimmie, Morris, and Sisley, was too busy to wonder about his kids' friends. Mela had tried to keep up. But if she was honest, she had had a challenging time too, balancing her demanding job as Rob's manager and being present for her kids.

She'd figured the kids were okay until Sisley had shown up in Bay Harbor scared and pregnant. Nobody had known the baby's father, Lars, had been abusive. It was scary to think what could have happened if he hadn't dumped Sisley to return to his native Norway.

Now that she had made time for family and friends, Mela still struggled with the fact that she hadn't noticed much earlier how much Sisley had needed her help.

"Anyway." Peter squinted out the window. "Advertising isn't going to help much until the tourists return next summer."

"You don't want to wait until next summer to turn a profit. And fall is beautiful here at the coast," Mela said distractedly. "It's too cold to swim, but there's long walks on the beach and fishing and foliage and fogs...and there's the farmers market." She looked up and grimaced.

She mostly tried not to think about the farmers market.

It attracted people from all over and was the town's one hot commodity—so hot, in fact, that Mela had been unable to get a stand to sell her honey. It'd been Julie's and her dream to have that stand. Unfortunately, the market committee was run by assertive ladies who did stellar work and didn't care about dreams.

"If we could only convince people it's worth making the drive, I think they'd love the town," Peter mused.

"But it's harder to advertise charm than whale watching."

"We need a photographer," Mela decided. "We need ads that show what they're missing when they pick a chain hotel in a crowded town over a...a boutique motel."

"Boutique motel?" Now Peter grimaced.

"It sounds better than Mom-and-Pop."

He grinned. "Mom-and-Pop? Who? Us?"

A faint arpeggio drifted like a fading sunray in the air, and Mela tilted her head. "Is Morris still playing piano?"

Of her three kids, her musical son, the middle child, had taken the longest time to visit Bay Harbor. But when Morris finally came, he came to stay.

His jazz band had split up.

It wasn't about the money, though the band's bookings had been his main source of income. Mela had known right away there was more. Morris was too depressed, too downcast, too stubbornly lost in his music. Bands split up all the time. Driven by talent and calling, Morris had always simply pivoted and formed a new jazz band or given more classical concerts. People paid good money to listen to him, and they paid even better money to play with him.

Careful so as not to spook her artistic male child, Mela coaxed the real reason out of him.

His good friend and the band's drummer had died of a drug overdose. Morris had been there when it happened. He'd tried to help, but there was nothing he could do other than watch the horrific scene.

For weeks, Morris spent his time playing the grand piano he'd had wheeled into the motel's dining room. Mela watched him closely, determined not to make the same mistake she'd done with Sisley and let him slip into darkness. But though Morris was shaken, he wasn't helpless, and though he was sad, he wasn't morose. He seemed very fond of his baby niece and bit by bit would sacrifice more piano time for the privilege of wiggling Lovie in his arms.

"He's been playing non-stop since this morning." Peter listened too, following the rapid-fire scales. "The boy's good."

"I think he calmed down. He used to be pretty wild, and I worried about him and his suitcase-in-hand lifestyle." Mela fell silent again. Of course, Morris had done more than drink coffee while his drummer overdosed. But he'd not shown signs of drug abuse since he'd arrived and swore unprompted never to have taken more than occasional recreational drugs.

Peter nodded. "I'm keeping an eye on him. He really is doing well. We don't exactly have heart-to-hearts, but we do spend a lot of time together. I often go and sit in the dining room, just to listen." He smiled. "At first, I didn't think my company mattered. But now I think it does. He warmed toward me. He's a good kid. I'm proud of him."

"I am, too." Mela smiled. "Thank you, Peter. I'm grateful for everything you do for him. For the girls, too. They have started to rely on you. I can tell. I can tell it makes a difference, too."

"I'm hoping by sticking around that Sisley will lose some of that fear in her eyes." Peter sighed. "Not sure I'm helping much there, though."

"It doesn't hurt." Mela sighed too. It was its own kind of painful to see how little trust Sisley had left in men—or her judgment. Neither her father nor her partner had kept their promises, and both betrayed her trust. Now she struggled to see what was true and what was false.

Bennett was true. But Mela couldn't tell Sisley, because it wasn't something words could sort out. At least not a mother's words. Mela's job was to listen and be there for Sisley. The last thing she wanted was to risk alienating her youngest daughter.

Of course, the hormones didn't help. Hormones never seemed to help.

A car arrived, the revving engine sounding through the open door. Mela leaned over to see who had pulled into the courtyard. "There you go. It's Sisley."

She stood and went to the door to wave. "Hello, darling! How are you?"

"Good!" Sisley slammed the car door shut and came to meet her. "Hi, Mom. You look great. Sorry I missed you this morning."

"Everything all right?" Mela hugged her daughter. Sisley and Mela's former assistant Johanna had moved into Kimmie's house. It was only a couple of houses down Seasweet Lane from where Mela and Sunny lived, but now and then an entire day went by without them seeing each other.

"Everything's all right," Sisley assured her and blew Peter a kiss. "Lovie's napping in your house, and Sunny's happily making more apple pies than you can store."

"We can always give them to the neighbors."

"What neighbors?" Sisley took the club chair beside her. "Oh. These are comfortable."

The two houses between Mela's and Kimmie's had stood empty since Mela returned to Bay Harbor. "Well, friends and acquaintances then," Mela conceded.

Peter nodded. "I think the younger Mrs. Botrel, who runs the Maison de Mer home goods store, would like a nice apple pie. She said her Breton mother-in-law makes too many fish dishes for her taste and that she can only sneak out to eat at the local café so often before Madame gets suspicious."

"Why not just tell her mother-in-law she doesn't like fish?" Mela raised her eyebrows. "Seems a difficult way to live your life."

"I think the younger madame adores the older one and doesn't want to hurt her feelings."

Sisley laughed. "Not sure an apple pie is going to help very much, but let's definitely give her one. And also the real estate agents, Kelly and Ian. Lauren, Kelly's sister... She runs the pizzeria, Mom. And maybe—"

"Let's see what Sunny has to say before you give them all away," Mela said mildly. "She might plan on keeping a pie or two for herself."

Sisley laughed. "I know more neighbors in Bay Harbor than I met in the years living with Lars. It's nice. I like knowing who lives in town."

"Keep at it. I read those small interactions are the most important thing in predicting how long you'll live," Peter mentioned. "Short little chats and all that."

"Like talking to the person at the supermarket register?" Sisley asked.

Peter nodded. "And the mailman, or even just waving thanks at a person who lets you go first at a stop sign. Apparently, being kind really makes you healthier."

"Maybe that's why it feels so good here," Sisley said. "People are really...uh. Kind." She frowned, suddenly distracted.

"Everything okay?" Mela asked casually. Something was bothering her daughter. Like Julie, Sisley needed peace and harmony.

"Yes...oh, I just remembered. Look what I found in the attic, Mom." Sisley pulled out a small photo. It was matte black-and-white, with brown spots speckling the sepia-colored backing. Judging from the poor quality of the photo, it was from the seventies or eighties.

Curious, Mela took it. A man, playing on the beach. "Who is this?"

"Let me see." Peter reached over the counter, and Mela handed him the old photo. "I've seen that guy before," he murmured. "But I can't place him." He handed the photo back to Sisley.

"Let me see again." Mela held out her hand, and Sisley returned the man in the swim trunks to her. "That face... Is that your dad?" she asked and held up the picture for Peter to look at.

Peter burst out laughing. "Maynard? He didn't own swim trunks. I promise you that."

"No. Of course he didn't." Mela and Peter had recently learned that after the death of his wife, Maynard had turned to alcohol—and violence. He'd beat Charlie after the boy took Amelie to the prom, cracking two of his ribs. That night, Charlie ran away. Unfortunately, Amelie's dad intercepted his letter to Amelie, and Charlie never learned she was pregnant with his son Bennett until he visited Bay Harbor thirty years later.

"It's not Maynard. It's a man called Finn Sullivan." Sisley straightened her back.

Mela stared at the picture. "Uncle *Finn*? Yes, you're right. I think I can see it. Only..."

"Only it should be Finn Palmer, not Sullivan. Look at the name written on the back." Sisley pointed at the picture. "At least that's what Sunny said."

"She's right. Finn Palmer." Mela turned the photo around and saw the name scribbled on the back. "Sullivan... He wouldn't have married and taken his wife's name, would he? No. Men weren't likely to do that back then."

"Don't you know?"

"He was only around in the summers. He took me to fly kites on the beach, and a few times he bought me ice cream." Mela tried to remember more. But she'd been so little, and it was so long ago... She could barely remember his face and had no recollection at all of his voice. There was mostly the feeling that he'd been nice.

Sisley cleared her throat. "Sunny also pointed out that *her* name isn't Palmer *either*."

"What? Are you saying Constance had another illegitimate child? No way." Peter raised his eyebrows.

Mela frowned. "I think giving up Sunny seriously affected my grandmother. She wouldn't have done it twice. And she had only Julie's picture in the drawer of her nightstand. I didn't see a single photo of Finn." She paused. "I mean, ever. There was nothing. It was like Constance didn't know Finn."

"Nobody had photos of anyone, though," Peter remarked. "Remember those little flashlight-cubes you had to pop on the camera? And the film you had to fiddle in and out of the things? Let alone bringing it in to develop them, and then half the time something went wrong anyway. What a pain that was." Despite the harsh words, he sounded nostalgic.

"I have a handful of photos of Mom, though," Mela murmured.

"Those are all from Bay Harbor," Sisley pointed out. "There's not a single one of her as a child. Who knows what Constance did with her photos? Maybe they're still in the attic. Julie might've taken them when Constance died."

"That would be something." Mela would love more pictures of her family. She fanned the picture at Sisley. "Where exactly did you find this again?"

"In a random box. It was stuck to the back of one of Julie's books. You know, from school."

"From school?"

"There were other books in there too. She tossed a bunch of things in. I didn't dig through all of it."

"Too dank?"

Sisley nodded but didn't look at Mela. "My dust allergy was acting up. Anyway—now I want to know more about Finn Sullivan. Uncle Finn."

"My uncle, your great-uncle." Mela wondered why Sisley wanted to know about him. Mela was curious too—but Finn had been her uncle. Sisley was another step removed, and she'd never met the man. Maybe it was her uncanny connection to Julie?

"Great-uncle sounds so stiff." Sisley slipped the photo back into her pocket. "How do I go about finding out who he is?"

"Ask Bennett," Peter suggested. "My nephew should be able to help. Identifying Does is his jam."

"Mm-hmm." Sisley looked down at her hands and blinked rapidly.

Mela's heart sank. When he was around Sisley, Bennett looked like the farm boy promising his princess bride true love. But her daughter was thoroughly done with men and wanted nothing less than another relationship. After being powerless for so long, she needed full control of her life.

They'd all waited with bated breath to see what would happen. Both of them couldn't get what they wanted.

"Did you two fight?" Mela asked gently. "You and Bennett?"

"No." The answer came too quickly. "No. I just... He's busy. And it's not that important."

"He *is* busy," Peter confirmed. "There's been a break-in at the jeweler's in Sandville, and they put him on the case."

Mela was unclear on how police departments worked. "I didn't know they needed homicide detectives for break-ins?"

Peter smacked his lips together. "They do for this one." He pointed his chin at the morning newspaper next to the computer. "Bennett will have his hands full until they catch the guy."

"Oh no," Mela said, alarmed. "Was there a shooting?"

"I'm afraid there was more than just a shooting." Peter flipped the newspaper over as if he didn't want Mela to see the headline. "The poor jeweler. He was only doing his job."

Sisley shook her head as if she didn't want it to be true. "But Bennett helped me in the attic this morning."

"There's not much he wouldn't do for you, kiddo." Peter smiled. "He was only put on the case a couple of hours ago. He called me because he needed me to pick up his nana Meredith for him." He sighed. "Playing canasta again. I had to wait until she was done. It took forever."

"He must've gotten the call as soon as he left," Sisley murmured. "I hope he'll be okay."

Peter's smile dropped, and he frowned. "I hope so too. Can't say I like him chasing the heavy guys. But don't worry, he'll be all right. We have to trust he knows what he's—"

Mela interrupted him with a loud cough. The color had drained from Sisley's face; she was as pale as a flounder's belly. "*Of course* he'll be okay. He knows what he's doing," she said heartily—more heartily than she felt—and took Sisley's hand. "This is nothing compared to that big case he had in Cape Bass."

"*Oh.*" Sisley pulled her hand away and covered her face.

"You *did* have a fight," Mela concluded.

"No. We just had a...a breakup. Without being together first."

Peter straightened. "Did you... You didn't... The poor m—"

"It'll be okay," Mela interrupted Peter again, shaking her head at him. The girl looked as if she thought her rejection had sent Bennett to his certain death. This was not the time to tell Sisley she messed up. Though frankly, everyone had been rooting for Bennett on this one.

"Oh, Mom."

"It's his job," Mela tried again. "Whatever happened between you two, this is what he *does*."

As if the words cracked a dam, tears started spilling from Sisley's eyes. "But what if something happens to him?" Her voice sounded as flat and smooth as ice. It scared Mela. "And the last thing I did was tell him he couldn't... I couldn't... I mean, we never really said, but I—"

"It's all right!" Mela pulled her daughter into her arms. "It's fine. You're fine. Of course that's what you had to say. It was the right thing to do, letting him know how you feel. It's not your fault he's got the job he does."

"What if he's distracted now?" Sisley whispered.

"He's too professional for that," Peter chimed in. Mela gave him a grateful glance. "He knows what he's doing. He went off on a job after meeting his long-lost dad, and he didn't let it faze him."

"You don't have to date him, and you don't have to put your life on hold because he's chosen a dangerous career," Mela confirmed. "Trust him. He's even better than you give him credit for."

But that had been the wrong thing to say again, and Sisley started to cry in earnest. Mela tightened her hug, widening her eyes in a what-do-I-do question at Peter, who helplessly shook his head that this was not his department.

"I'm so worried," Sisley sobbed. At least her voice was full of snot and hiccups instead of icicles now. "Bennett—and I haven't heard from Kimmie in so long. I hate that we can't reach her."

Mela froze. She had not been able to get in touch with her eldest either. Kimmie was a journalist and part of an investigative team researching human trafficking in Tucson. Mela knew little more about her eldest's job than that it was incredibly dangerous and would cross Kimmie's path with the worst of the worst.

"We'll call Kimmie's editor tonight," she said, forcing her voice. "He'll know where she is."

CHAPTER 5

Kimmie pulled her black silk robe closed at her throat. She hadn't switched on the light once in her NYC apartment since she returned from Tucson. Now it was night outside. And though the city never slept, dark still huddled on dark. She stepped forward to see better. Dressed as she was, nobody should be able to spot her this high up, even if she was standing at the window.

The streets below were never truly empty. Sometimes, when late night faded into early morning, there was a space—an hour or two—where no one was visible on the pavement when you glanced outside. But there were always eyes like hers, glancing out from dark windows. There were always people, even if they didn't show themselves.

Kimmie glanced at the watch that glowed on the desk. It was barely eleven now. The owners of townhouses and apartments were leisurely strolling home, relaxed and chatty after dinner and a glass of wine. Others, the enthusiastic, younger crowd, probably only left now to catch dinner at a club. Lost tourists from Jersey or Ohio, who'd strayed too far from the glittering lights of Broadway, stared at maps on phones, swiveling them as they tried to find out where north was, or the way back to Penn Station, or the bus depot on 42nd.

Kimmie turned away. Nobody lingered. Nobody stood under a streetlight in designer jeans or gang sneakers, furtively glancing up at her apartment.

The danger had passed.

She was good.

She picked up her phone and weighed it in her hand. Mom would be worried. Kimmie had missed the last time she'd agreed to check in, and nobody had her new phone number. Kimmie didn't take her old phone to assignments like the one in Tucson. She couldn't risk Mom calling at the wrong time or in the wrong place. And if she lost the phone and the people running the ring hacked their way into her contacts...life as she knew and enjoyed it would be over.

So Kimmie left her treacherous old phone in Bay Harbor and took a burn phone the newspaper provided. It meant that nobody could get in touch with her; only the editor had the number, and he knew better than to call.

But all that was over.

Kimmie's cover had been blown when someone recognized her on the street while she was chatting up one of the handlers. An old college buddy of hers who'd beamed and slapped her shoulder and asked what the heck she was doing in South Tucson and was she still living in NYC. Hey—maybe she got a job as a journalist at the University of Arizona? Would he see her more often now? And who was her lovely friend? Hand outstretched and smile wide, a friend meeting a friend of a friend.

Kimmie had hooked her arm firmly under her buddy's and whisked the two of them out of the situation and into the car she'd had idling at the curb out of sheer dumb luck, and then she screeched out of there. Before the handler, young and pretty as she was, could pull her gun and shoot her and her buddy down.

She'd never met anyone as cold as the people running the ring.

Kimmie shivered and stepped farther away from the window.

It'd been two weeks since she returned to NYC. She'd dumped her college buddy at a busy street corner and drove the one hundred-ninety-three miles to Show Low, Arizona, because of a gut feeling someone would be waiting for her at the airport in Phoenix. She hadn't called anyone, hadn't let anyone know where she was so nobody could be made to tell.

In the weeks since her return, her nervous system had calmed down again. She couldn't go back to Tucson for a few years. Not even close. But she could go to Bay Harbor now. And she could call people again. The imminent danger was over. The ring didn't have time to waste, and if they knew who or where she was, they'd have taken care of her already.

Kimmie went back to her laptop; the only glow in the apartment came from the open screen. She read what she'd written, corrected a few sentences for clarity, typed out her note to the editor, and then she pressed *send.*

She had done her part. The rest was in the hands of her editor.

Time to relax and rest.

Kimmie put the newspaper's phone into a manilla envelope and sealed it, then went into the dark bedroom and sat on her bed. The silk of her robe rustled against the satin of her sheets, and suddenly, she wanted cotton.

She wanted cotton and sun, salty breezes and open doors. Her mother, her sister, and her aunt. Mussels gathered at dusk instead of Chinese takeout delivered to the door.

She wanted Bay Harbor.

Kimmie's hand trembled with relief when she pressed the key.

"Kimmie? Kimmie, is that you?"

"It's me, Mom."

"I was so... Are you all right?"

"I'm all right. I couldn't call, but I'm all right. I'm sorry, Mom. I'm fine."

Her mother inhaled air the way someone who drowns inhales water; wet and panicky. "Where are you?"

"I'm back in the city."

"Oh thank heavens." A deep exhale, and another. "Are you done? Why are you back?"

"I'm done." Kimmie sank on her back and closed her eyes. "A friend accidentally blew my cover, but we made it out of there before they could react."

"They know who you are?"

"Maybe they can face-match me, but I doubt they have a picture of me."

"What does that *mean*, Kimmie?"

"They don't know who I am," she explained. "They might realize I'm not who I claimed I was." Kimmie didn't say that she'd tried to infiltrate the ring. It was the only way to get in touch with the victims.

"What now?" Mom asked. "We're all worried because we couldn't get in touch with you. Sisley cried today."

"Because of me?" Kimmie pressed her lips together.

"Uh. Partly."

"And the other part?"

"Bennett."

It made Kimmie laugh. She hadn't laughed in ages. "Still a no from Sis?"

"Yes, only this time Bennett won't be back, I think. We'll see."

"Tell her I'm fine. How is Lovie-Dovie?"

"Thriving. She gets bigger every day."

"And how are you, Mom?"

"Perfectly worried about you, Kimmie. What's next?"

"Bay Harbor, I think." Kimmie rested her forehead in her hand. "I want to stay for a while. Water my plants, go swimming. My nervous system needs a reset."

"Please come and stay." Suddenly, Mom sounded close to crying. "Come here. Johanna found work as an online PA. Maybe you can write essays or a column for a newspaper. Or I'll buy them off you if you let me."

Kimmie laughed again. "I'll write you something nice," she promised. "But it'll cost you."

"Fine. As long as you're safe. When can you be here?"

Kimmie pulled the cashmere coverlet over her feet. It wasn't cotton or linen, but at least it wasn't glassy silk. "Tomorrow," she said sleepily. Already she could tell this would be her first restful night. "I'll be there tomorrow night. It's a seven-hour drive, eight with city traffic. We'll have dinner together, okay?"

"Oh." Mela swallowed. "Yes, Kimmie. Please come. I'll make..."

"Matzo ball soup."

Now Mela laughed. "Matzo ball soup? Really?"

"That's all I want. I've been craving it for days now. It's warm and comforting."

"All right. I'll make a second course too, just in case."

"Mussels? Out on the patio? With the twinkle lights?"

"If you like. It's getting colder in the evenings."

"I like. Mom, I'm falling asleep. I love you. I'll text you when I leave. Oh. Let me give you this number. You can call me now." She texted the numbers.

"Thank you, Kimmie. You have no idea how relieved I am."

"See you soon." Kimmie yawned, and then the phone slipped from her hand, and the call ended.

She was drowsily gazing at the blue glow of the screen, ready to doze off, when the phone rang, startling her awake. Nobody had called her since she got back.

She grabbed it. "Yes?"

"Kimmie?"

Sleep made her slow. She blinked. "Who is this?"

There was a moment of silence, and suddenly, she was scared that they'd found her after all.

"It's me. Travis. You said... Gary told me you were working on a project with him. He said I could call."

"Travis." Kimmie elbow-scrambled into a sitting position. Her robe slipped open, and she grabbed the coverlet to cover herself as if a stranger had suddenly appeared in her bedroom.

Because that's what her ex-husband had become. A stranger.

After their silent divorce, they'd talked exactly once. Travis had left Kimmie to care for Tina, a woman with whom he'd had a one-night stand before he met Kimmie and who'd been injured on the job.

"Is this a bad time?" Travis asked.

"No." Kimmie ran a hand through her short hair. "What's up?"

"I wanted to let you know..." He hesitated.

Kimmie waited. Like her, Travis was a world traveler and journalist. If he needed a moment to tell her something, Kimmie needed that moment too.

"I wanted to let you know that Tina has died," he said finally. "She passed away from her injuries. They never got a handle on the infections, and, well...it happened a couple of weeks ago. I—couldn't call sooner."

"Oh." He didn't have to tell her at all. "I'm so sorry, Travis. I really am." Kimmie's heart constricted as she thought of the other woman. Tina had been a talented photographer. After learning Travis had left her to be with Tina, Kimmie looked up some of her work. She'd liked it. There'd been beauty and dignity in her photos.

"You don't have to say that." Travis sounded uncomfortable.

"I mean it," Kimmie replied. "I saw her work. I would have liked to know her. Of course I'm sorry. What happened to her was terribly unfair."

"I was going to ask if...and you can say no, Kimmie. Please."

She tilted her head. "You know me, Travis. I'll say no if I want to. Ask away."

"I was going to ask if I can take you up on your offer."

Kimmie blinked. "My offer? My offer to..."

"You invited us to come to Bay Harbor. You said...you said it was a place of healing, and we desperately need some healing."

"Of course. I remember now. You can come any time, Travis. I'm not... I'm in NYC right now, but I'm driving to Maine tomorrow. I'll meet you there."

"Yeah?"

"Yeah. We'll have coffee and walk on the beach. If you like. Or...or you can be on your own. I told you the invitation wasn't to get back together."

"I know," he hastily fell into her words. "It's very kind of you. Especially after the way I handled the divorce. I shouldn't have—"

"No worries." It was Kimmie's turn to interrupt him. "None. It's fine. That's all done and over with. The past is the past. We moved on."

"The thing is..." He sighed. "I'm not coming alone."

"You're not coming alone? Are you—" Kimmie stopped talking. A dog? A new girlfriend already?

"I'm bringing my daughter," Travis said quietly. "If you'll have the two of us."

"Your—" Kimmie couldn't breathe; the words snatched the air from her lungs. Travis had a *daughter*?

"Her name is Pippa," he said. "She's mine, and the reason Tina put me in as her emergency contact."

When Tina had been shot in a drive-by shooting, the hospital had called Travis first. When she learned this, Kimmie had wondered why a one-night stand had meant so much to Tina—and Travis.

Kimmie should've guessed. Of course she should've guessed. Suddenly, not guessing seemed like hiding under a soft blanket. She'd done it as a kid. If she couldn't see the truth, she didn't have to deal with it. "Oh," she said scratchily. "I see."

"I swear I only learned I had a daughter when I went to see Tina in the hospital. I wasn't supposed to know Pippa existed," Travis said. His voice was scratchy too, as if telling the truth was no easier than hearing it. "And Tina wasn't supposed to die and leave Pippa."

"She had your baby, and you didn't know? You didn't know when we got married?"

"Of course I didn't know, Kimmie. I didn't know until Tina was shot. She had no choice but to tell me."

"So it wasn't only Tina who needed you to take care of her." Kimmie needed to say it to understand it.

"Pippa needed me too. And...Tina wanted to make sure she was...still there while Pippa got used to me. She..." He couldn't go on. He inhaled shakily.

"Travis."

"Yes?"

"Come to Bay Harbor. You and Pippa can stay at my house. Sisley and a friend of mine, Johanna, live in the house, but that's good. They'll take care of everything so you can concentrate on your kid. There's one big bedroom you two can share. I'll stay with Mom."

"Oh. No—I thought you said the house was empty. I'm sorry. I wouldn't have asked had I—"

"Travis, it's a good idea to come to Bay Harbor. I want you to come. I want both of you to come." Kimmie closed her eyes. "How old is Pippa?"

"She's four."

"I have a baby niece." Kimmie smiled. "She's a month old, and her name is Lovise. Pippa and Lovise, that's pretty cute. We'll change so many nappies we won't have time to walk on the beach."

"Walking," he repeated as if dazed. "I don't know when I last took a beach walk."

Kimmie quieted. "Was it hard, Travis?"

He started crying, and she waited for him to get out his grief and his tears. It was a while before he said, "The hardest thing I've ever done, Kimmie."

"Bay Harbor is a good place for a new beginning," she said gently. "When can you come? You'll have to fly into Boston and rent a car."

"I can leave tomorrow," he said. "Now that she's gone, there's nothing to keep us in England. If we take a red eye, we'll be in Boston around noon."

"I'll be on the lookout," Kimmie said. "My mother promised to make matzo ball soup. Does that sound good?"

The sound he made belonged in the land between crying and laughter. "I *hate* matzo ball soup."

She smiled. She knew he didn't like her favorite comfort food, always complaining the matzo balls were too mushy and he wasn't a toothless infant. "Give me a call when you land. And tell Pippa..." Kimmie swallowed. The man who used to be her husband had a child. It was still strange. "Tell Pippa I'm looking forward to meeting her."

"Thank you, Kimmie. You're..."

"You too, Travis," she whispered when he couldn't finish. "You are, too."

She ended the call. Then she got up and started packing. If she left right now, she'd be in Bay Harbor for breakfast.

There was a lot she needed to do to get the house ready for a grieving man and a lost little girl.

CHAPTER 6

The truck pulled to the curb in front of the house, casting shade on the geraniums that were blooming, red and luscious, in the window boxes.

Amelie leaned against the door jamb and crossed her arms.

When she'd lived in the house, the geraniums never bloomed in October. October! It was too late in the year for anything but asters.

"Aren't they great?" Amelie's mother, Meredith, stepped beside her, nodding happily at the riot of color.

"They're very red," Amelie replied politely.

Meredith smiled and patted her arm. "I appreciate that you kept them alive all these years, darling."

"You're welcome." Amelie smiled back. She'd never liked the geraniums; they were too alpine for the Cape Cod house, and she couldn't stand the scent. But her mother loved it.

The truck door opened, and the driver climbed out, checking a bunch of papers in his hand and pulling a pencil from behind his ear.

She sighed. "You had a two-bedroom condo in Florida, Mom. Where is all this stuff coming from?"

"Mostly the storage unit. Good morning." Meredith greeted the driver and scribbled her signature where he pointed.

"Where do you want the boxes?" The driver waved to his passenger, who opened the door and jumped out.

"Into the living room, please."

Amelie handed the man a generous tip. "Thanks very much," she said. "I'm grateful I don't have to schlepp any more boxes."

The man tucked the bills away and grinned. "It's what I do." He nodded and went back to the truck. The other man had already opened the back and rolled out a ramp and trolleys.

"Let's go inside," Meredith said and blinked at the sky. "I'm cold." She shivered and rubbed her arms as if she was standing knee-deep in snow.

"It's warm today, Mom." Amelie followed her mother out of the bright October sun into the old family home. It hadn't been the happiest home, and while Amelie had lived in it for almost all her life, she was glad for the beautiful new house Charlie had given her. The gift had come at the perfect time. After learning her grandson was moving to Bay Harbor, Meredith had suddenly decided to do the same.

Amelie loved her mother, but she didn't need to live under the same roof. They were too different, their relationship too complex for that to be a good idea.

"Do you want a drink?" Amelie asked the men when they brought in the first tower of boxes from the storage unit.

The driver who'd gotten out first nodded. "Coffee would be great if you have it. We've been driving through the night, and there's not been a single Starbucks or a Dunkin' Donuts ever since the last rest stop on the highway."

Amelie smiled. "We don't have many chains here. Give me one minute, and I'll brew a fresh pot. Have you had breakfast yet?"

The man pushed his cap back and glanced at his friend.

The friend shrugged. "Not really, if I'm honest. But don't put yourself out. Maybe you can tell us where there's a good place to eat in town."

"Nonsense." Meredith waved the comment away like a bothersome fly. "There's plenty of food in the house."

Amelie nodded. "You're in for a treat," she told the men. "Nobody makes better breakfast than my mother."

After running a bakery empire for years, feeding friends and family—and strangers, strays, and anyone else who looked peckish—had become second nature to Meredith.

The men mumbled something about no trouble, but Meredith had already left for the kitchen, where she pulled pans and pots from the cupboards. "Amelie, do you remember how to make scrambled eggs?" She shook back the fluttery sleeves of her dress.

"Do I remember how to make scrambled eggs?" Amelie crossed her arms. She was known for her cooking skills in Bay Harbor. She'd gotten prizes at the local fair. Her mother wasn't the only one born with a talent for making tasty foods. "Yes, Mother. I do."

"Well, I know you can make scrambled *eggs*." Meredith narrowed her eyes. "But can you make them the right way?"

"I make them *my* way," Amelie replied coolly. "And they are delicious."

"You have to whip them separa—"

"Thank you," Amelie interrupted. "I got this."

To her surprise, her mother chuckled. "Of course you do. You're almost fifty, aren't you?"

"I am. And you are almost seventy and therefore should know better than to throw little darts," Amelie said. "What's with that dress, by the way?"

"I *like* it. That's what. I got many compliments on it in Florida." In a flurry of ruffles, Meredith turned to pull a pack of bacon from the fridge and slap it on the counter. "Why? Don't you like it?"

Amelie turned to study her mother.

Something had happened in the years Meredith spent in Florida. She was different, not as uptight. The low bun, pinpoint earrings, polo shirts, and belted pants of Amelie's childhood had given way to flowing gray hair, chandelier earrings, frilly dresses, and bare feet.

"I think you look fabulous," Amelie said and rounded the kitchen island to hug her mother. "You look like a crazy chick from the beach."

"Thank you." Meredith hugged her back. "I was going for artistic, but crazy works too."

"Let's start over." Amelie pressed a kiss on her cheek and went to get the eggs from the fridge. "I'm looking forward to getting to know the new you, Mother."

Meredith turned on the flame under her pan and peeled slices of bacon apart. "I'm still the old me too. Some bits got thrown out of the window, though."

"On purpose?" Amelie inquired while cracking open eggs. Her dad had run the family business into the ground and lost what was left to his gambling addiction. Meredith had to reinvent her life when she least expected it.

"On purpose." Meredith put the bacon in the pan, where it started to sizzle and fill the air with the scented promise of a hot breakfast. "I drifted along to someone else's beat too long. I should never have given the reigns to my fortune over to your father."

Amelie didn't reply. She'd already been out of step with her family when everything came crashing down around them.

Meredith looked over her shoulder. "I'm all right, darling. Maybe it needed to happen. To be honest, I'd been dreaming of divorce for years. Sad as it is, I'd never have gotten up the courage to leave if it hadn't been for that call."

Amelie remembered the call. It was a wonder they'd managed to keep the house.

She whisked more air into the already foaming eggs and poured the liquid into her pan. "I'm mad, but I understand." She pushed a spatula under the egg and started to scramble them. "Do you think Charlie's letters might be in one of the boxes from the storage unit?"

"If I have them, they're in there," Meredith answered and drained the last bacon rashers on a paper towel before pushing the plate into the oven to keep warm. "But darling—I doubt Charlie ever wrote them in the first place." The shock of finding her barely graduated daughter pregnant—and the father a man she'd explicitly been forbidden to date—had rattled Meredith.

"I think you should meet him," Amelie said and scraped the cooked eggs in a bowl. "I think you would like him."

"Well. Can you make waffles? I'll start a pot of coffee and cut fruit."

"Yes, Mother." Amelie whipped up the dough in her favorite bowl and wisely stayed silent while she baked the waffles in her mother's heart-shaped waffle iron.

Whatever her parents thought, Amelie had truly been in love with Charlie. And now...she still liked him now. That was all she needed. Her mother's approval would be nice, but Amelie wasn't eighteen anymore. She could be friends on her terms.

For a while, they worked in silence.

"That looks nice," Meredith said finally and nodded at the stack of waffles Amelie was dusting with powdered sugar.

It was a peace offering, and Amelie took it. "I have cherry compote to go with them."

"Bacon and eggs, waffles with cherries, fresh fruit, coffee... How about the cinnamon crumble muffins you made last night? Think they're still good?"

Amelie smiled. Heir to a long line of bakers, Meredith needed her baked goods to come fresh from the oven. "They're not even a day old. Let's put them on the table, or they won't get eaten. Bennett complains of getting fat. He's used to his detective's diet of instant ramen and apples, not home cooking."

"Bennett could never get fat," Meredith said loyally. "He's so handsome."

"He is." Amelie chuckled. Much as her mother detested the father, she adored the son.

They loaded the table and called in the movers, who introduced themselves as Sam and Benno and happily helped themselves to food and coffee while they talked about their drive and their work.

Meredith picked at a waffle. "You didn't happen to see a box labeled with a big cross, did you?" she asked.

"I did, actually," Benno said. "I just carried it in. It's next to the fireplace."

Amelie looked up. A box with a big cross? "Dad's things?"

Meredith let her waffle be. "Whatever is left of it," she said. "I threw most of his things away, but I didn't know what was in these boxes, and frankly, I couldn't be bothered to check."

"I'll have a look." Amelie, too, had lost her appetite. She poured coffee and chatted about Maine and the coast and how beautiful it was up here, but her thoughts were with the contents of the box.

Charlie had sent her twenty-five letters explaining why he had run away and asking her to join him. Amelie had never gotten a single one, and the shock of finding herself abandoned and pregnant had eroded much of her trust. If Dad had intercepted the letters and she could read even a single one to see Charlie was telling the truth, it would change everything.

She looked up. “Is it okay if I take Dad’s box home with me?”

Meredith waved a tired hand, the chunky rings on it weighing it down. “Please do,” she said. “I wasn’t going to look at it. It’ll be all old, unpaid bills.”

“Excuse me.” Amelie nodded at Sam and Benno and stood. “I have to take care of something.”

She found the box and lifted it without difficulty. Her heart sank. Whatever was in it was light. Letters didn’t weigh much, but what were the chances her father had held on to them? He’d detested Charlie.

As Charlie had said, he’d been from the wrong side of the tracks in the eyes of many people. Amelie thought the description better described her father than Charlie, but maybe that was the exact reason Dad had felt so strongly. It took one to know one.

Mom came into the living room. “Did you find it?”

Amelie nodded. “I’ll see you later,” she said, cradling the box.

“Let me know,” Meredith said. She hesitated.

“What?”

Meredith shook her head as if she couldn't believe she was saying this. "I do hope you find your letters." The corner of her lips twitched in a tentative, doubtful smile, and then she turned and left.

"I love you too, Mom," Amelie said, then she hitched her box higher and went home to see what she would find.

CHAPTER 7

Sisley shook her hair back. She was wearing the warmest dress she'd found in Grandma Julie's closet—an ankle-length maxi with a pattern of tiny brown flowers that went well with her blond hair and the light tan the beach had given her.

"Everything all right down there?" she whispered to Lovie, who was snuggled up in the sling, and kissed the downy head. Lovie, fast asleep and sucking on her tiny fist, made a snuffling sound. "Me too," Sisley agreed and eyed the door to the Beach Bistro. "Let's go in."

She pushed open the door and stepped inside the small restaurant. There were still tables outside, but the sea breeze tugged on hair and clothes and whirled red, orange, and yellow leaves through the air.

It was easier to talk when there was no wind.

Heart drumming, Sisley let her gaze wander over the tables. Two of them were pushed together by a group of seniors and laden with coffee cups and big plates of hot apple pie slathered with melting whipped cream and vanilla ice cream. The seniors were slapping cards on the table and laughing raucously.

The third table, away from the seniors, was taken by a single man.

Sisley took a nervous breath and fixed a smile on her face.

She couldn't stand having him be mad at her. Maybe he could forgive her. After not sleeping a wink, she intended to find out. Bennett was not Lars. Maybe she could smooth over the feather she'd ruffled.

Bennett looked up, and when he spotted her, he stood. Nervous, Sisley weaved her way past the tables, waving at the card players she recognized and nodding at the server, Lucy, who smiled back and pointed to a stack of coffee mugs. Sisley nodded yes, and then she reached Bennett.

"Hello," he said formally. "I'm afraid I don't have much time, Sisley."

So they would get right into it. "Hi, Bennett," Sisley said. "Is there enough time for a cup of coffee?" Already, Lucy was balancing one, biscuit on the saucer, over to them.

"Yes."

"Hi, Sisley. How's my little snuggle bug?"

"She's asleep." Sisley took the coffee. "Thanks very much, Lucy. I'll make sure to stop by to say hi before I leave."

"Got it." Lucy cast a curious glance at Bennett and left again to take up her station by the register.

"What's up?" Bennett asked. His cup was empty already. He'd come early. Or he'd downed scalding hot coffee. One of the two.

"I wanted to make sure we're okay," Sisley started before she could chicken out. She wasn't good with conflict. She liked harmony and peace and hated when someone was upset with her. But during her long, sleepless night, she'd decided to learn how to deal with conflict instead of avoiding it. She took a breath. "I hurt your feelings. And I want you to know that I love you." She stumbled over the last word. That's *not* what she'd meant to say. "As a friend," she added hastily, feeling heat shoot into her cheeks. "I mean, I love you as a friend."

A smile twitched his lips, but it didn't spread. He pushed his cup aside and leaned forward. "And what if that's not enough, Sisley?" he asked. "What if I want more than being friends?"

Lovie stirred and croaked like a frog, stretching her little arms so the hands showed. Sisley started to rock her. Bennett closed his eyes, and then he opened them again with a sigh. "Can I see her, please?"

Sisley nodded, tongue-tied, and wiggled the baby from the sling, handing her to Bennett.

"Hey there," he murmured. Lovie blew a spit bubble and blinked at him.

"I don't know what to say, Bennett." Sisley eyed the pair. Bennett was perfect in every sense. But she simply didn't want to be in a relationship. Not now. Maybe never. "I'm not looking for anything more than what we have. Can't we just stay friends?"

He looked up briefly before Lovie reclaimed his attention. "We've never really been friends, Sis," he said casually. "It's always been more, don't you think?" He cradled Lovie in the crook of his arm. "I love you, Sisley," he said quietly. "I know it's real. How about you? How do you feel about me?"

Sisley's cheeks were dry with heat. She glanced at the senior table beside them. The lady closest to them had fallen quiet, her ear pointing in their direction.

Well—it wasn't a secret. Sometimes it seemed as if all of Bay Harbor was rooting for them to become a couple.

"You're my best friend," Sisley whispered firmly. "But I can't love right now, Bennett. The feeling scares me. I just got out of a troubled relationship, I have a newborn, I just moved here... I can't take on more. I can't promise anything. I'm sorry."

He nodded, lifting Lovie just enough so she could kick her legs. "No need to be sorry. At least now I know."

She exhaled. "So we *can't* be friends?" She heard the note of despair in her words and pinched her lips shut.

He glanced up. "That's something *I* can't promise. I've never thought of you as a friend."

"Okay. Fair enough." She took a sip from her coffee, just to get over the moment. It'd be hard to live in Bay Harbor without being friends with Bennett. "Can we at least stay civil?"

He frowned. "Why wouldn't we?"

Because whenever Lars had been mad, he'd yelled. Said hurtful things. Called her names. If his words were knives, he'd have drawn blood, letting her bleed out over and over.

Sisley shrugged. The memory was enough to harden her resolve. "I'm sorry, that was... Of course. So...can I ask you something else?"

He picked up his napkin to wipe the burst bubble from Lovie's cheek. "Maybe." His voice was tightly contained, his eyes on the baby as if he would never see Lovie again.

"This new case you're on...is it safe? Are you safe?"

Now he looked up. His forehead crumpled into a frown. "Why do you even know about that?" He shook his head.

"Everybody knows, Bennett," she said timidly.

"Aha. Well, I'm as safe as always," he responded. "I'm a cop, Sisley. It is what it is."

"Okay." Sisley was starting to sweat. She stood to slip off the silk sling that was still warm from carrying Lovie and sat again, crumpling the beautiful fabric on her lap. She couldn't stand Bennet being so distant. "Please be safe."

He shook his head once. "No offense, but I hardly need your advice on how to do my job."

"It's not advice," she murmured. "It's a request. I couldn't stand it if you got hurt. Despite everything."

"Well, despite everything, I have to do my job." His lips moved as if he wanted to say something more, but then he stood. "Talking about it, I have to get back to work."

Sisley nodded and stood too. She thought Bennett would hand back Lovie, but he still cradled her in his arm. The baby was falling asleep again.

Bennett looked down at her, and then his face softened. "Well, I do have two more minutes, I suppose. She'll be cranky if I wake her up now."

"Oh."

They sat again.

"I'm always careful, Sisley," Bennett said. "Don't worry on my behalf."

"Mm-hmm. Oh. Um. Do you remember my mom's Uncle Finn?" Sisley asked.

"He was the one with the boat. My mother told me about him. Shady guy, if you ask me."

"Shady? How shady?"

"Didn't he build the boat that killed him and your grandmother? What was her name?"

"Julie," they both said at the same time, Bennett answering his own question.

"Yes, Julie," Bennett repeated. "Why do you ask? What about Finn?"

"I found a photo of him," Sisley said and pulled up a snapshot of the photograph on her phone.

"I'd really like to know what happened." Bennett studied the face.

"Here's the back," she said and swiped to the shot of his name. "Finn Sullivan."

"Ah," Bennett said. "Back when they labeled their photographs."

"The thing is," Sisley said eagerly, glad to keep him a little longer, "his last name should've been Palmer. Like his sister Julie. But here it says Sullivan. See?" She tapped on the screen, enlarging it. "Finn Sullivan."

"Hmm." Bennett tilted his head.

"Well, Sunny said maybe he's another adopted kid, just like her. I was wondering whether you could look up the name. It'd be good to know who he was or where he came from. Mom said Grandma Julie didn't write much about him in her journal. Isn't that strange?"

Bennett's expression hardened into a professional mask. "I'm sorry, I can't do that. I don't look into private persons. And you shouldn't either."

Sisley drew back. "He's my granduncle," she said, hurt at the sudden change in him. "And he died at sea. Why should he remain faceless? How would you have liked Sunny to stay in the motel, never knowing she had a niece and an entire family in town? Of course I should try and find out more."

"Leave it be." Bennett stood and, despite his earlier protestation, lifted the sleeping baby off his arm. "Here. I have to go." He handed Lovie to Sisley, nodded once, his eyes already on the exit, and walked away without another word.

Sisley was stunned.

"You all right, Sis?" Lucy had come to the table, and Sisley hadn't even noticed her coming.

"Oh. Yeah." Sisley tried to smile. She didn't know Lucy too well, but they chatted every now and then when meeting in town. "Yeah. He had to get back to work."

Lucy frowned at the door. "It's only, he hasn't paid for his coffee."

"I'll pay for it," Sisley said hastily. "It was on me today." Bennett never let anyone pay for anything—he must be upset. Either he didn't like Finn, or he'd decided they were being too friendly again.

"That's not what I meant," Lucy murmured. "But he seemed mad. Was he rude to you? I don't mind telling Amelie to sort him out."

Sisley was so surprised she almost laughed. Small towns—everyone knew everyone else. Be rude in the Beach Bistro, and by afternoon your mother would set you straight. She stood. "No, he wasn't rude. He's just busy," she said, trying to sound calm and centered. "It's all good. I'll come to the register to pay."

"Yeah, I heard he's going after the guy who shot the jeweler. Never mind. The coffee is on the house. Here." Lucy helped her slip the sling back and nestle Lovie inside. The baby woke and squawked, dissatisfied with the switch from Bennett's arm to the sling. Lucy smiled. "Uh, you weren't counting on him for a ride, were you?"

"No, I wasn't." Unwieldy, Sisley pointed at her phone on the table. "Could you hand me that, Lucy?"

"Sure." Lucy took the phone, her eyes grazing the screen. "Finn Sullivan? He's...hmm. How do I know that name?"

Sisley tilted her head. "I don't know. How do you?" She swiped to Finn's face.

"Oh, hey." Lucy smiled fondly. "I know. It's the guy who runs the Candy Apple Store over in Beach Cove. I make sure to get one every time I'm over there. They're that good." She took the phone and squinted at it. "Is that him as a young man?"

"I don't know," Sisley repeated, nonplussed. "Does it look like him?"

"Kind of." Lucy returned the phone. "I only know him from buying his apples, but I think his last name is Sullivan. If you want to know, you could just drive over there and ask. He's pretty nice. But do it sooner rather than later. He's pretty old."

The senior with the open ear cleared her throat loudly.

"Pretty old," Sisley repeated absentmindedly. "How far away is Beach Cove?"

"Like a short hour," Lucy replied. "You can drive along the coast, though, and the street takes you up the cliffs for a view before it dips down again. Take a real map. It's a cute little town, but your phone won't work. They need an extra radio tower or three over there."

"Maybe I'll go," Sisley said and tucked her phone away. "Truth be told, I don't mind getting out for a bit."

"Aha," Lucy muttered, throwing a dark look at the door through which Bennett had vanished.

"If I go, I'll bring you a candy apple," Sisley promised and pulled out her wallet. "What do you like?"

Lucy smiled. "I like the chocolate ones with caramel and walnuts. Coffee's on the house."

"What if I don't go?"

Lucy patted the bump Lovie made in the sling. "Don't worry about it. Let me know how it goes."

"Well, thank you." A little embarrassed, Sisley tucked her wallet away. She didn't want to insist. Already, the seniors were focusing more on her than their cards. "I'll see you, Lucy."

"See you." The bistro phone rang, and Lucy left to answer.

One of the senior ladies leaned into Sisley's path as she was leaving. Her wrinkled face told Sisley that she was at least in her eighties, if not older. "You're Pamela's girl, aren't you?" the woman asked in a scratchy voice. "Julie's grandchild?"

Sisley stopped. "Yes, I am. I'm Sisley."

"I'm Candice. Can I see your baby? She's so pretty."

"Sure." Sisley folded the sling down so that Lovie's head appeared, eyes wide open, rosebud lips pursed curiously.

"Oh, she's gorgeous," Candice murmured and reached for Lovie without touching her. "If you ever need a babysitter, come by my house. I babysat your mother, not that I expect she'll remember it."

Sisley smiled. She had plenty of babysitters and wouldn't leave Lovie with someone she didn't know well, but it was a kind offer. "Maybe we can take her to the beach together sometime," she said. "That would be lovely."

"That *would* be lovely," Candice confirmed. "Listen. Was Amelie's boy nice to you? He was mumbling into his beard an awful lot. I can always talk to Amelie, you know. Nobody's rude to a young mother on my watch."

This time, Sisley couldn't help but laugh out loud. It was the second woman ready to march up to Amelie and complain about Bennett on her behalf. "On the contrary, he was very polite," she said. "If you do see Amelie, tell her I'm very fond of her son."

Candice nodded, satisfied. "You two would make a great couple," she said, turning back to her cards. "I was telling Marissa here before he stormed out what a pity it was you are single. You should think about it."

Sisley straightened the fabric to secure Lovie. "How do you know I'm not married?" she asked, unable to help herself.

Candice looked up, surprised. "I thought he went back to Norway?"

Sisley didn't know if she should laugh or cry. "But how do you know that?"

"How do I *know* that?" Candice smiled. "You haven't lived here long, have you?"

"I just moved here a month ago," Sisley admitted.

Candice nodded. "Everyone knows everything, child," she declared, and then Marissa complained she was holding up the game and not to frighten the poor girl and to concentrate.

Sisley left. When she stepped out of the door, she saw the seniors from both tables bend their heads toward Candice, eager to catch her words. Even Lucy was watching from the register, arms crossed, listening in.

"Oh boy," Sisley muttered, feeling equal parts amused and alarmed, and let the door swing shut behind her.

CHAPTER 8

Sisley would have quite liked a sweet candy apple to calm her nerves after her talk with Bennett, but Lovie had had enough. By the time Sisley parked the car at the house, Lovie, usually the happiest baby anyone could ask for, was screaming at the top of her voice. She had slept enough and wanted to move, not sit strapped into her baby carrier and stare at the boring back of the car seat.

With every high-pitched protest, Sisley felt her nerves frazzle more. "Lovie, we're home!" She jumped out to get her baby out of the car. "I'm so sorry, you're so good, we're all right, almost in the house," she babbled as she fished baby and sling and seat and diaper bag from the car, juggling everything to the house.

Unable to get to her keys because her arms were full, she pushed the doorbell, hoping Johanna would be home.

Johanna was home. The door opened, and there she stood, laughing when she saw Sisley. She grabbed the car seat and sling and bag and stepped aside so Sisley could come in.

"Ooh nooo," Johanna cooed and set the jumble of things down to take the screaming Lovie. "Are you hungry, little mouse?"

"She is *so.*" Sisley got rid of her purse and phone, feeling sweaty and out of breath. "I'm afraid I pushed it out too long."

Johanna handed Lovie back. "Better nurse her quick, mama. I'll make us a cup of peppermint tea." She stretched. "I've been working all morning. My eyes are going to cross if I don't get away from the screen for a moment."

"Tea sounds lovely. Thank you, Jo." Sisley went into the living room.

When Kimmie left, there'd been barely any furniture in the house. Between Sisley and Johanna, Amelie and Mela and Meredith, everything that was needed to make a home cozy had since been supplied. There were new down couches in the living room, wicker poufs, and sheepskin rugs that went with the hazelnut-wood-and-white-brick theme. Johanna had developed a thing for oversized potted plants, and they filled the corners in their pretty wicker baskets, turning the rooms into spa-like oases.

With a huff of gratitude, Sisley sank onto the couch and started to nurse while Johanna was energetically clanging pots in the kitchen. Sisley smiled. Johanna was doing much better than when she'd first moved to Bay Harbor after her mother's passing. Her depression had lifted, and she was back to her usual adventurous self.

By the time the tea was ready, Sisley was burping Lovie on her shoulder.

"Here you go." Johanna set the mugs on the table when the doorbell rang. "Hang on."

Lovie finally burped, and Sisley spread a quilt on the floor and sat beside it, laying Lovie on her belly so she could practice lifting her head. Her neck muscles were getting stronger every day, but she would still need a month or two before she'd be fully able to control her head.

"Look who came to visit," Johanna said, bringing their tall visitor into the living room. A new light shone in her eyes.

"Morris! Don't tell me you were able to tear yourself away from the piano?" Sisley asked. Her attempts at getting him out of the motel had been largely unsuccessful.

Morris ran a hand through his unruly hair. "I know, I know, sometimes I am like that. But I suddenly had a burning desire to check on my niece. See what she's up to—and you, too." He sat beside her.

"I'm honored. Hi." Sisley leaned into her big brother for a moment, letting him know she appreciated it.

"Peppermint tea, Morris?" Johanna asked and pointed to the second mug. "Have mine. Freshly made just a moment ago. I haven't drunk from it yet."

Morris shook his head. "Thanks, but you go ahead, Johanna. Why don't you sit down? I've barely had a chance to talk with you."

Johanna hesitated for a moment, but then she joined them on the floor too. "All right."

For a while they watched Lovie lift her head and drop it again. Morris put his hand between her head and the quilt so she wouldn't hurt herself.

"I heard you were asking Mom about her uncle Finn today," he mentioned eventually. "The one who built that boat."

"Yes, I found a photo of him." Sisley showed him the photo and repeated the story of how she'd found it. "I've gotten a tip that there's a Sullivan in Beach Cove. He runs the Candy Apple Store in a town not far from here. I thought I might drive over and say hi."

Morris looked up. "Alone? With Lovie?"

Sisley narrowed her eyes at the judgment in his voice. Morris wasn't the type to fuss over her safety. For years, he'd barely cared enough to show his face at family reunions. "Why not? It's a candy store." She heard the irritation in her voice and cleared her throat. What she really wanted was to connect with him the way she'd reconnected with Kimmie.

"I'll go with you," Johanna said quickly. "Don't worry, Morris. Kimmie told me to keep an eye on them."

"Oh please." Sisley shook her head and turned Lovie onto her back, pushing Morris's hand away. "You all don't need to treat me like I'm an idiot. I can handle making some friendly chit-chat over an old photo *and* caring for my baby. Besides, is there anything safer than a candy store?"

Morris looked past her at Johanna. "I'll come too," he said casually. "It'll be fun to drive along the coast. Candy apples are my favorites."

"You *don't* like candy apples," Sisley said, exasperated. "What is this? How stupid do you think I am that I can't do this on my own?"

"I think you're very smart, in your own special way." Morris grinned and caught her hand when she swatted at him, tossing it back at her as if it was a glove. "Kidding. I just like the thought of taking a drive and seeing the coast." He looked at Johanna.

Sisley turned to protest and saw that Johanna was holding her brother's gaze. Her cheeks had a rosy tinge that didn't look like it came from drinking peppermint tea.

"Oh. Okay," Sisley said slowly. This wasn't about her safety at all, was it? "We'll all go together. Have a fun trip." With her as the third wheel...

"But not today," Morris said, finally breaking free. "Kimmie's coming home."

"*Kimmie's* coming home?" Sisley felt her eyes widen. She put a hand to her throat where a lump of worry had lodged itself the day Kimmie left Bay Harbor. "How do you know that?"

"She called Mom. Mom's told me to tell you."

"When?"

"Last night."

"And you're only telling me now? Morris!"

"I thought you needed your beauty sleep." He grinned an apology.

"Did you know, Jo?" Sisley looked accusingly at her friend.

"Kimmie texted half an hour ago," Johanna replied, dodging the question. "I thought she'd let you know too."

Sisley snapped up her phone. "Oh no. I clean missed it. It must've come when the seniors were so loud I couldn't hear my phone. And then I was busy with Lovie."

"What seniors?" Morris asked, but Sisley only murmured, "In the bistro," busy reading the few words her sister had sent. "Kimmie should get here any minute." She looked up, alarmed. "We need to get the house ready. We need to vacuum and wash the towels, and I want her bathroom clean, and her bedroom needs to be...*aired out*." She inhaled a deep breath. She'd been so worried about Kimmie! "I'm *dizzy*!"

Johanna laughed. "She's fine, Sis. I already opened the windows in her room, and I even whipped up a batch of her favorite cookies, though I'm sure Sunny's busy cooking up a storm."

"Towels?" Sisley pulled her knees to her chest. She couldn't tell whether she was dizzy with surprise or relief.

Morris laughed. "I didn't know you were so fond of Kimmie."

Johanna made a clucking sound. "There are plenty of towels, and the floors are always clean for Lovie anyway. It's all right, Sis."

"Looks clean to me," Morris murmured, running a hand over the plush white sheepskin rug.

"Do you know more?" Sisley pointed a finger at Morris as if it were a gun, forcing him to give up all his information. "She isn't injured, is she?"

"No, she's fine." Morris picked up Lovie and stood, rocking her. Lovie made small, content sounds, her eyes on her uncle's face.

"Okay." Sisley watched her brother.

He was good with his niece. The years since leaving home seemed to have tamed him, and the seaside air had given him the sheen of health that had been missing when he first arrived. Mom and Amelie fed him regular meals, and Peter and Bennett managed to get him away from his music now and then, teaching him useful skills like fixing vintage truck carburetors and properly preparing a nice pot of Earl Grey.

"Is Kimmie going to stay this time?"

"How would I know?" Morris looked surprised that she would ask him. "I have barely exchanged five words with her since she moved to New York."

"Are *you* going to stay?" Sisley held her breath. She'd not dared to ask before. Morris shrugged, but again she saw him glance at Johanna.

"Would you answer if *Johanna* asked you?" she asked, only half kidding. Morris had a bad track record with girls. Even in school, he'd been a heartbreak who enjoyed his title.

"Sisley!" Johanna stared at her, but Morris only smiled.

Sisley raised her hand in a question. "What? He keeps looking at you when I ask him something."

"Would you like to go out with me, Johanna?" Morris inquired. "I and my little sister need to know."

"Tell your little sister it's none of her beeswax." Johanna's cheeks had gone from faint blush to carmine. "Uh. No."

"No?" Something in his eyes made Sisley stay out of it. Her intuition had got it right. Had she been so involved in her baby and her affairs that she'd missed Morris falling for her housemate? When had the two even met, other than during family dinners?

"I...am going to close the windows in Kimmie's bedroom," Johanna declared, avoiding the siblings' eyes. "Byeee. And you're not allowed to talk about me behind my back." She hurried away, leaving her tea untouched.

"That wasn't a no, Morris," Sisley said earnestly when she heard her friend rattling the windows upstairs. "Better be careful."

"I'm not careful by nature, Sis," he replied, just as earnest.

"She's a good person, and she's only just getting out of a rough time. Her mother passed away. Don't mess around with her if you aren't serious. Mom will have your head. Me too. Kimmie too."

"Who says I'm messing around?" He held out a hand, and for some reason, Sisley took it. He pulled her to her feet, then handed her Lovie. "Maybe I'm done with all that, Sis."

"That would be...a change," she said carefully. "And I'd love it, Morris. Just realize that Johanna doesn't have many people to fall back on. Us, really. So if it gets awkward between her and this family, it would be unkind."

Morris put a hand on her shoulder. "I'll keep that in mind."

Sisley brushed off his hand and turned away. He was starting to annoy her. "I'm not kidding. Stop being sarcastic."

"I'm not. I'm serious. Look."

Sisley did. His eyes were open and honest, but she'd known Morris to lie and look like he couldn't harm a fly. "Morris, for real."

"For real, Sis. I'm done with all that."

"Define *that*." She tilted her head. Never before had he said he was done—but then, they'd not talked much at all since he moved from their childhood home in New Hampshire.

"Women." He shrugged, suddenly looking exhausted. "I'm done waking up next to someone I don't know. I'm done waking up next to someone I don't like." He inhaled. "Drugs, if you want to know. After Kenny... I'm clean. It took a while." He cast her a glance. "But I'm doing it."

"Morris." He'd never admitted what she'd been wondering for years. She held out a hand. "Really?"

"It was never the hard stuff." His fingers gripped hers. They were warm and long and effortlessly elegant. Like hers. It was the one thing they had in common.

"You never tried it out?" It was too good to be true. The company he kept, the places he went... Surely he'd tried harder drugs?

"Once or twice." He shook his head as if he was annoyed with himself for it. "Afterward I couldn't play the way I wanted to. I learned to take only enough to take off the edge. That's how it started. Then suddenly, taking that pill or drinking that nightcap wasn't my choice anymore. And then Kenny died. I asked him to stop long before that happened." He ended abruptly and cleared his throat. "After that, I realized I'd been starting down the same path, so I checked myself into a facility. It took a while, and it wasn't easy. But I'm all right now."

"I had no idea. I wish you'd talked to me. Or Mom. Maybe we could've helped."

"You would've been worried. I couldn't carry anyone's worry; I could barely handle my own. There literally was nothing you could have done other than make me feel even more terrible about my choices."

"We're so different," Sisley said. "Your support would have been everything to me if it'd been me going through something like that."

"Everyone in the center was dealing with it their way." He looked out the window at the softly rolling sea. "For myself, I had to do it on my own. But honestly, coming to this cute little town..." He smiled at her. "It's pretty easy to focus on doing the right thing here. I'm not trying, but I doubt I could get in trouble here even if

I wanted. Besides—correct me if I'm wrong, but I think your Bennett is keeping a close eye on me."

Sisley exhaled; she didn't want to talk about Bennett. Not now, when Morris was opening up. "It does take focus. Well..." She let go of his hand to adjust her hold on the baby. "Okay. If you're serious, you have my blessing. I mean, when it comes to Johanna."

"All right then. Thank you, Sisley." His smile turned back to the old teasing grin. "I wouldn't want to ask her out without my baby sister's blessing."

"Ask out who, Morris?"

They both wheeled around. "Kimmie!" Sisley called, and before she knew it, her sister was hugging her and Lovie, and then Morris was embracing them both.

Finally, Kimmie had come back to Bay Harbor.

Chapter 9

Mela took the chain of twinkle lights from Sunny and wound them in the branches of the old apple tree. Then she stepped off the wooden box and surveyed her handiwork.

Tonight, she wanted everything to be perfect.

For the first time in forever, she had all her kids together. Tonight was going to be the beginning of something new and wonderful. She went back on the box to tug the chain over a higher branch, then put it back where it'd been.

"It's good," Sunny said, sounding exasperated. "Stop fussing."

"I'm not fussing," Mela said automatically. "I just want it to be nice. Kimmie's back. Morris—I can't even remember Morris showing up to a family dinner."

"Hmm." Sunny checked her new smart watch. "I need to clean the mussels."

"I thought we said lobster." Mela felt alarm rising in her chest. "We said we'd make *lobster*."

"Oh dear." Sunny put her hands on her hips, and for a moment Mela wondered whether her mother Julie would have looked like her sister had she lived to old age. "Of course we'll make lobster. I was going to *also* make mussels in white wine sauce. With garlic. Kimmie loves mussels. And I don't know if Morris even likes lobster. Not everyone does, you know."

Mela breathed a sigh of relief. "Of course he likes lobster. Do we have garlic bread?"

"Ready to go into the oven. And I was going to make fries. Kimmie was talking about how they eat fries with their mussels in France. I thought it wouldn't hurt."

"So we have garlic bread, mussels, lobster, and fries?" Mela had to laugh. "That's quite the mix."

Sunny grinned back. "I got fresh oysters and grilled shrimp too, if you have to know."

"What if someone just wants a burger?"

"Well, too bad. They'll have to wait until it's burger time. Or they can fill up on dessert. I made strawberry ice cream earlier."

"Yes, I heard." The churning of the ice cream maker was only tolerable because the ice cream with its little bits of half-frozen strawberry chunks was delicious. Mela had tasted it before, and it was a great addition to the feast. She put an arm around her aunt's shoulders and squeezed. "Thanks, Sunny. I wouldn't know what I'd do without you."

Sunny made a doubtful sound. "Fuss more, I suppose. Well, come on. Mussels, and let's get the tables set up too. I don't know why you had to set everything up in the orchard." She shook her head. "The patio would have been good enough."

Mela leaned her head back to look up into the gnarly branches. High up, where neither Sunny nor the deer could reach, still hung apples. Red and luscious, they scented the fall air. "I want it to be special. It's the first time all the kids are here. I'm so...*so* happy, Sunny."

The old lady beside her softened. "I know," she murmured. "I know, honey."

Mela pulled herself together. "Let's switch the lights on. I want to see how it looks."

"You won't be able to see anything; it's still too bright."

Mela had already turned toward the honey barn. "Oh come on, I just want to make sure it works." She plugged the first chain in the extension cord and looked up. "Oh!"

The afternoon was bright, but the leaves on the trees shaded the branches and the lights twinkled like fireflies, their glow reflecting on the shining apples. "That's pretty."

Sunny only nodded.

"Oh, you like it!" Mela laughed and unplugged the chain again. "Just wait until tonight when we'll sit under the trees with the lights between the apples and the stars above and the sea rushing in the background. You'll cry; it'll be so beautiful. I knew putting the table in the orchard was the right call."

Contentedly, she surveyed the folding tables and chairs Peter and she had brought out earlier. She would push the tables together to turn them into one long one. She had scored a couple of beautiful blush linen tablecloths at Maison de Mer that would turn the humdrum tables cheerfully festive. Amelie had helped pick thick bouquets of pink and blue asters and clouds of white fleabane, and she was going to come over for coffee and cake while they arranged them in cheerful little vases to scatter over the table. "Oh! I still have to take the price tags off the charger plates," she remembered suddenly.

"Is that what those green wicker things on the kitchen table are?" Sunny asked. "Charger plates?"

"Yes. They'll be gorgeous."

"What sort of dishes?"

"The white ones from the attic. They have little roses. It'll be cute."

"Not two things on that table are going to be the same color."

"That's the point. Nothing matchy-matchy. Like my kids."

Sunny chuckled. Now that the twinkle lights were off, she'd found her feet again. "Well, knock yourself out. I'll clean those mussels."

"I'll start on the tablecloths and clamps while I'm here." Mela went to the bags she'd stored by the honey barn when she spotted Amelie walking across the grass toward them, waving.

"Hi!" Mela took out the tablecloths and waited for her friend to arrive.

"Hi!" Amelie hugged her. "This will look gorgeous, Mela. I hope it won't be too windy."

"The forecast is good. You never know this close to the sea, but...fingers crossed."

Sunny stoically accepted Amelie's kiss on the cheek. "Don't you make Mela even giddier than she already is," she warned.

"How's the hip? Do you enjoy walking?" Amelie smiled at her.

"Oh." She'd caught Sunny off guard. "It's the best." She cleared her throat. "I have to clean...the mussels. Excuse me." She walked off, one hand on the new hip as if she wanted to make sure it was still there.

Mela chuckled. "It's so much better. She's a whole new person. Still grumpy when I get emotional, but a heart of gold. Mostly."

Amelie laughed. "That's all we can ask for. It's kind of her to do all the cooking for tonight."

"It really is," Mela confirmed, keeping to herself that Sunny wouldn't share the task at gunpoint. "Are you here to help? It's earlier than you said."

Amelie shrugged. "I had to get out. I'm going crazy going through Dad's old papers. How he could be so irresponsible with his gambling...I'll never understand."

"It's an addiction," Mela said. "You worked through that, didn't you?"

Amelie gathered a handful of clamps and followed her to the table, where she dropped them on a chair and helped spread the tablecloths. "I guess. I'm just speechless that he squandered my mother's fortune the way he did. Not a care in the world."

"It is hard to accept," Mela agreed. She knew Amelie didn't like talking about that messy time of her life. Mela straightened to see her friend's face. "I meant to ask—what happened to Charlie's letters? Did you find them?"

Amelie shook her head. "Not in that box. I don't know what's in all the boxes that went into the guestroom. I guess there may be another one with Dad's stuff. It can't all be Meredith's old shoes, can it?"

"I have no idea."

Amelie looked up. "What?"

"Does it really matter?" Mela asked. The breeze picked up, and she pushed a strand of hair back. "Does it matter whether he sent those letters?"

Amelie smoothed out the blush fabric. "I suppose not."

Mela pinched a clamp on the table to hold the cloth in place. "What happens if you don't find them?"

Amelie scooped up a few clamps and started to snap them in place. "Nothing, I suppose. It's just... It'd be nice. To know for sure."

"Let's say you find them."

"Yes?"

Mela realized her friend wanted to hear her say that it didn't matter whether Charlie had sent her letters. Even though Mela's opinion shouldn't matter, after all the years of thinking he'd abandoned her, Amelie had not yet come to terms with it.

Mela straightened. "Let's say you do find them," she repeated softly. "Would it make a difference?"

"Doesn't it?"

"Thirty years after running from a father who broke his ribs and scared the daylights out of him, he's come halfway around the earth. To see you."

"He was homesick." Amelie looked at her, unsure whether Mela could convince her.

"Your house was the first place he visited. He never forgot you. I promise, Amelie, the man has thought of you every day for thirty years. He never married."

"No." Amelie nodded. "Like Peter never forgot you."

"Whatever else they are, Townson men are loyal," Mela said. Peter had had relationships, but he'd never loved anyone the way he loved her. Even if his father, misguided as he had been, had loved his wife more than anything. When she died, his life had spun out of control.

Amelie blinked. The wind was tugging on her tunic blouse. "Has Peter asked you yet?"

Mela shook her head. "He knows me too well. I don't think I'll ever marry again."

Amelie smiled. "It's too early after your divorce to think about marrying."

Mela had loved Peter ever since she'd been ten years old, even if it had taken her forty years to see it. And yet she couldn't imagine a good reason to get married. "I don't think so. I'm happy with things the way they are. I like living in my little house with only a crotchety old aunt for company."

"Aww, you should tell Sunny. She'll be so flattered. But I suppose you're right," Amelie added loyally.

Mela had to smile back. "What I meant to say is...why should it matter whether Charlie sent the letters? He was only a baby. And so were you."

"I don't know, baby," Amelie said and snapped a clamp in place. "We were old enough to... you know. *Have* a baby."

"But why should how Charlie felt back then matter more than how he feels now? Besides, he'd only just finished school. His mom had died, his brother had left him, his dad beat him, and he had to juggle all that on top of graduating. You were all he had. I'm sure he *adored* you. You were the light in his life. Letters or no."

Amelie pressed her lips together. "I'm already sorry enough for him. You don't need to take his side."

"There's no side. He had to run. He's never forgotten you, and he traveled around the world to find you. He's bought you the house of your dreams. And more importantly, he's obviously over the moon to have Bennett for a son. He's everything..."

Amelie looked up, one eyebrow raised. She tugged the last bit of fluttering tablecloth tight. "Everything what?"

"Everything you ever wanted?" Mela opened her hands. "Or why have you never found anyone else either?"

"So you don't think it matters if he's lying?"

Mela pinched her lips, considering her words. "No," she finally decided. "I don't think it matters. I think he truly loves you."

"Well." Amelie had used the last of her clamps and had nothing left to do. "It's very sweet of you to try and convince me of it. For what it's worth."

Mela finished too. "What do you mean, for what it's worth?"

Amelie blew out a breath. "He lives in *Australia*, Mela. What I do or don't believe doesn't make a difference."

"Call him," Mela suggested. "Even if you don't find the letters, give him a call. If you want..." She shook her head. "We're getting older, Amelie. Why not ask for what you want? Call him and ask him to come back to Bay Harbor."

Amelie's throat moved before she spoke. "Don't egg me on, please. I can't take on that responsibility. What if he comes back and we don't get along?"

"Of course you get along," Mela said simply. "You belong together. Give your man a second chance. If anyone deserves it, it's him. He's gone through enough, and you know you're the only one for him. Why not embrace love while we can? Forget the stupid letters."

Amelie bowed her head. "I don't know," she mumbled, but Mela heard the words in the wind.

Suddenly it was as if they were beamed back in time to the years they never spent together, when Amelie graduated from high school in Bay Harbor and Mela drifted through the foster system. Suddenly it was as if they got to relive a moment in their friendship they had missed before.

Mela went to her friend and embraced her. "Amelie," she said into her hair. "Let's do what we couldn't do back then. Let's say yes to love."

Amelie's shoulders twitched, but when Mela let her go, her eyes were dry. "I wish you'd been there with me," Amelie said. "I really needed you."

Mela inhaled as a wave of memories swelled inside her, threatening to darken the golden October afternoon. "My mother should never have disappeared back then. All of it was so...so *wrong*."

"I wish Julie could be here with us." Amelie's eyes did tear up, and she swiped an impatient hand over them. "Mela, we better get it together."

Without warning, Mela's thoughts flew to Sisley and the way her youngest resembled Julie. "We have Sisley," she tried to rally. But it was too late. The sunlight seemed a little dimmer, her joy at the family party a little less exciting.

"Ugh, Mela." Amelia shook her head. "Look at us, making ourselves miserable. Let's go and have a glass of prosecco and a piece of the raspberry cream roll I brought. We'll look out at the sea and think of Julie until we feel better again."

"There's still so much to do," Mela said. "The flowers need to be put in vases."

"Forget the flowers," Amelie replied. "Your kids aren't going to care a crumb about flowers if you start crying. Come on. Cream-roll time."

She hooked her arm under Mela's.

"Fine. I'll go, but only if you call Charlie," Mela said. "Only if you tell him finding the letters doesn't matter."

"Maybe I will."

"And you ask him to come back."

Amelie threw her free hand up. "What is this? The relationship police?"

They started walking toward Julie's house. "If I'd been able to stay in Bay Harbor back then and knew you were looking for him, we'd have found him," Mela promised. "I'd have figured out where he was."

"Oh sure," Amelie groaned. "And I didn't because I was too stupid."

"Maybe you were too hormonal. Baby brain is real."

They bickered and haggled their way to the patio, where they convinced Sunny to stop chopping garlic and come out to share the raspberry roll and the afternoon sun with them.

Slowly, they joked their way back out of the old hole Julie had left, and by the time Peter and Bennett joined them, they had once again gained solid ground under their feet.

Only now, the ground felt a little different than before, the soil worked once more with friendship and tenderness and forgiveness.

Mela thought it possible that with soil like this, even the deepest holes could be filled.

Chapter 10

Kimmie wiped her mouth on a napkin that had happy little clam shells on it. She knew she should only dab at the corners, but the lobster had been too juicy and buttery to pretend elegance. On her right, Mom was telling Bennett about the food license she got to sell the honey from her bees and how the competition for stands at the Bay Harbor Farmer's market was so full she still couldn't get one.

On her left, Sisley was sweetly singing Lovie asleep with a lullaby. Bennett was nodding to Mom's story but had his eyes on Kimmie's sister while Morris was boring Johanna with an endless explanation of something musical. Jo graciously asked a bunch of questions to keep Morris happy. Peter had assigned himself the task of refilling glasses with wine and in between was reading vineyard labels to Amelie, who was tipsy, and Sunny kept cutting into conversations, trying to get everyone to take another scoop of steaming mussels, another piece of grilled rosemary-and-garlic bread, just one more succulent lobster claw.

The day's blue hour was melting softly into a night as dark and sweet as a ripe plum, and a salty breeze tickled the branches of the apple trees, making the yellowing leaves above their heads dance and the stringed lights flicker like fireflies.

Sisley stopped singing, and Kimmie saw that the baby had fallen asleep. Her eyelids had fluttered shut, the long lashes lying like shadows on the round cheeks. The tiny fingers with their mother-of-pearl nails were tightly curled into fists. She'd snuggled them against her chubby cheeks on both sides, which puckered her rosy lips as if she was waiting for a kiss.

"I'm so happy you're back," Sisley whispered when she noticed Kimmie's gaze. "And so is your niece. She needs her auntie to spoil her. Or change her diapers. Whatever. As long as you're here."

"I'm happy I'm back too." Kimmie smiled. "There's nothing better than coming back to a house full of friends and family. I love my apartment in the city, but I have to admit it can be lonely."

"Good. I hope you sell that apartment and come live here for good." Sisley took a sip of grape juice that stood in for the wine she couldn't drink because she was nursing. "Was it terrible where you were?"

"Yes." Kimmie shook her head as if she could shake off the images she'd seen. "I'm glad it's over. I already sent in my piece, and I'll just let the editors do whatever they want with it. I won't go over it again."

"Bad, huh?"

"There's not enough water in the sea to wash it off. I never want to go into that. And uh...I couldn't anyway."

Tina had been shot in a drive-by shooting while working as a photographer. It'd been a random accident that had cost her life. If Kimmie went back, she doubted it would be a drive-by shooting for her. She picked up her glass to swallow the thought.

For a while, Sisley silently rocked Lovie. "Why did you go?" she asked finally. "You had such a good time here. Then suddenly you couldn't wait to leave. You said nobody else could do a job that needed to be done. That's not true, is it? There are plenty of good reporters out there."

Kimmie looked down at her hands. She'd had many occasions to ask herself the same questions while she was standing on dirty street corners and in even dirtier bars, trying to blend in with dirt-lot cacti and white-collar pimps when of course it was impossible. There were not only other reporters who were eager for the job but better suited than her. They didn't have friends in town to blow their covers.

"Yes," Kimmie admitted. "There are other people who can do it." Maybe her sister would leave it at that.

But Sisley was not so easily sidetracked. "Was it because of Travis you went? You left soon after talking to him."

Kimmie shrugged. "No," she lied. "The divorce was too long ago to matter." The correct answer, of course, was *yes*. But she wasn't about to admit it because first, she hadn't known herself, and second, she wasn't proud of running every time things got difficult. And with things, she meant her feelings.

“So Travis is coming here? It’s hard to believe after the way you guys left things.”

“He said he would.” As if her sister’s words had summoned him, Kimmie spotted Travis rounding the honey barn. Holding on to his hand was a small girl with sleepy eyes, messy hair, and a fluffy teddy bear that was dragging through the fallen leaves.

“There he is,” Kimmie heard herself say as she rose.

“Oh.” Sisley stood too. All the other faces gathered around the table turned, staring at Kimmie’s long-lost ex.

“Excuse me,” Kimmie said. What she meant was, carry on. This would be awkward enough.

“Ask if they’d like to join us,” her mother whispered as Kimmie passed. “There’s plenty of food.”

Kimmie didn’t have the bandwidth left to answer, only nodding mutely. Heat flooded her neck and cheeks, and she blessed the night for covering the evidence of her nerves.

“Hello, Travis,” she said when she reached him and was glad to find her vocal cords working. Over here by the barn, it was even darker than under the twinkle lights, and she could see him less clearly. His features seemed softer to her than before. He’d gained weight. Not much, but she was an expert when it came to the angles and planes and lines of his cheeks and jaw.

“Kimmie.” He looked at her with a ghost of that crooked smile she’d loved so much.

For a moment, it was as if they'd never been apart.

Then, Kimmie squatted so her face was at the level of Travis's daughter. "Hello, Pippa," she said and smiled gently. She could see Travis in the delicate pale features. "Are you very tired?" She picked a leaf from the teddy's fur.

The girl nodded, pulled the teddy away from Kimmie, and buried her face in it.

"It's been a very long day," Travis said, sounding relieved to have something to say. "We got up in the middle of the night. Pippa has slept in the car on the drive from Boston, but she's still very tired."

Mom joined them. "Hello, Travis," she said and held out her hand. "It's good to see you again."

He shook her hand. "I'm glad to see you again too," he said politely. Then his voice changed into something darker and more genuine when he said, "I'm very sorry about leaving as I did, Mela. I know... I didn't know what else to do. I'm sorry."

"I'm so sorry about what happened. I can't imagine." She glanced at the little girl who was studying her curiously.

"Thank you."

"We're so glad you could come," Mom said kindly, and Kimmie threw her a grateful look. Mom wasn't one to carry a grudge. Kimmie had told her what she knew, and by the end, her mother only seemed eager to make sure Travis's daughter would feel welcome. Pippa was not the only one who had lost her mother much too early.

"Thank you," Travis murmured. "I appreciate it."

"Kimmie will stay with me for now," Mela continued. She didn't try to engage the little girl, only smiled at her for a moment so she knew she was included. "You two will be in Kimmie's house. Does that sound good?"

Travis glanced at Kimmie, and she smiled back. "If it's not a bother, that'd be great. I'm sure Bay Harbor will be good for Pippa. We need a vacation, and friendly faces." He pressed his lips together and frowned. Kimmie thought it'd been a while since he had someone to lean on.

"Would you like to see your bed, Pippa?" she asked to give him a moment.

The travel-weary little girl, her face still pressed into her bear, nodded.

"She's shy," Travis said, a small smile tugging on his lips.

Suddenly, Kimmie wanted to hug him. But of course she couldn't. "Come on then," she said as casually as she could. "Are you hungry?"

"We stopped at a McDonald's for dinner," Travis said. "We're fine. But thank you."

"Maybe we can have lunch together tomorrow?"

"That sounds nice. If you're okay with..." Travis inhaled. "Sure. I'm sorry. I still feel like everyone in your family should be mad at me. You, in particular."

Kimmie saw him grip his daughter's hand firmer. He'd been overwhelmed when he got that call from Tina's hospital. He'd needed her, but she'd been traveling. Neither one of them was at fault. If they had worked together better, if they'd built better communication skills while they could, it would have been easier. But when in life wasn't that the case?

"Let's go," she said softly. "We can talk later when there's time and you two aren't falling asleep." She kissed her mother's cheek and murmured her thanks for the beautiful welcome party. Mom made a beeline back to the table, pushing a chair in between Amelie and Sunny. The three women put their heads together, and Kimmie smiled. No doubt they were already planning how to fatten up the new guests and put roses back on their cheeks.

"Let's go home," Kimmie said and automatically, without thinking it through, held out her hand for Pippa. The small girl, dazed with exhaustion, took the hand without a moment's hesitation. The bear dangled between them. Travis looked surprised.

"We can walk," Kimmie said. "It's faster than driving." She started to lead her guests into the soft night.

"I appreciate a night walk," Travis said. "I've had all the driving I can take."

"Did you rent a car at the airport?" Kimmie led them past the house and through the asters in the front yard.

Travis had rented the car at the airport, and it was a bigger SUV than he'd ever driven before, and between the two of them, they managed enough small talk to make it down Seasweet Lane to Kimmie's house. The lights shone warm and welcoming in the windows, beckoning them to enter. Kimmie pushed the front door open.

"Don't you lock your door?" Travis asked.

"Not here," Kimmie said. "Bay Harbor is safe."

He didn't reply, but she understood the doubt in his eyes anyway. For reporters like them, the concept of a truly safe place was as unlikely as a rainbow trout in the deep sea. "Trust me." She smiled. "You'll see. But I'll lock the door tonight, and I'll give you a key so you can feel comfortable."

She switched on more lights and the gas fireplace and brought them upstairs. The remainder of the first meeting with her ex-husband was taken up with the pointing out of rooms and towels, extra blankets, and bedside water.

They were to take her bedroom, which was big and had plenty of space to fit the small child's bed that had once belonged to Mom. Peter had carried it over earlier. Mom had also picked out and brought over a selection of her old toys, a few vintage clothes from the seventies in case Pippa didn't have what suited seaside life. Bennett had arrived with a crate full of his old kid books, though Kimmie thought Pippa, at only four years old, was more likely to know her way around an iPad than the alphabet.

Kimmie left as soon as she could. The travelers looked dead on their feet, and Pippa's eyes had started to glaze over as if she was sleepwalking. Travis formally shook Kimmie's hand good night, which of all the strange things she felt was the strangest yet. She locked the door as promised and walked back on her own to 12 Seasweet.

The houses in between hers and Mom's were dark, but here too, the lights in the house shone warm and inviting into the night. Kimmie let herself in. She could hear voices and laughter; the men were trekking back and forth between orchard and barn and house, bringing chairs and tables inside. The women were drinking wine in the kitchen and laughing and pretending to do the dishes while really only stacking them in the sink.

"Do you want a glass of Pinot?" Sisley had spotted her and held up a bottle.

"I think I do," Kimmie said. Suddenly, she felt as exhausted as her guests had looked. "How about you? Only grape juice tonight?"

"I just nursed, so I can have a sip," Sisley decided. "Do you want to go sit on the wall? It's nice and quiet out back."

"Yes please," Kimmie said gratefully.

Mom, having caught the exchange, nodded her approval across the room. Sisley grabbed clean glasses and the half-full bottle to bring.

They sat on the fieldstone wall, swinging their legs over the side so they could see the white crests of the ocean waves. Protected from the breeze by the trees, the night felt as smooth as velvet.

With a plop, Kimmie uncorked the bottle and filled the glasses her sister held out. Then she stored the bottle in the grass by her feet and deeply inhaled the spicy fragrance. "I missed the last of the fireflies," she sighed, exhaling again. "I always liked the fireflies."

"They'll be back next summer—here's to Bay Harbor's bugs." Sisley held up her glass, and even in the dark, Kimmie could see her smile. "And friends. And family too. Past and present."

"Here's to all that." Kimmie clinked hers to her sister's glass, making Julie's crystal ring like a small bell in the night. "You have no idea how glad I am to be back." She sipped, letting the warm notes of red fruit, flower and spice aromas roll over her tongue.

"Maybe I do." Sisley leaned, lightly resting her head on Kimmie's shoulder.

"Yeah," Kimmie said quietly. It was good not to be alone. Life was a big old ocean, but sometimes family could make it seem like a sweet summer pond. "Maybe you do."

CHAPTER 11

Amelie stood at her kitchen island, surrounded by trays of cookies and stands of cakes. The oven had been going all night, and the air was like a down blanket put on the bed before the heat of summer had properly passed. The scents of pumpkin and apple, cinnamon and nutmeg, and brown sugar wafted around her like friendly ghosts eager for attention. Amelie's cheeks felt flushed and dry under her floury fingers.

She opened the top button of her yellow linen blouse and went to open the sunroom door, fanning herself with her hand. Outside, the crisp air was still cool from the night. Amelie stayed a moment, admiring how the early-morning sun filtering through the rhododendron made the leaves glow emerald. They would stay all winter, too. Rhododendron didn't drop in the fall, so she'd still have something pretty to look at when the snow came.

It wasn't only the sunroom that made her happy. The whole house was beautiful.

She adored every room, every crook, every window seat.

"Happy about the sunroom?" Bennett's voice came from behind her, and she turned. Her son had come into the kitchen, fully dressed and with a newspaper under his arm, to get a cup of coffee before taking off.

"Always. Good morning, my dear."

"Good morning." He pressed the button on the coffee machine. "Did you have trouble sleeping?" He nodded at the baking that was stacked all over the kitchen counters.

"Yes."

"Anything on your mind?"

"Oh, I don't know. That little girl, Kimmie's girl—"

"Do you mean Travis's daughter? Pippa."

Amelie nodded. "She looked so tired and sad it broke my heart. I want to make her feel better."

"Well, if what she needs are cookies, she should be all right. You made enough for all of Bay Harbor," he murmured. "There's that."

"Of course she doesn't need cookies. But she might need people who care enough to bake her some. Are you in a bad mood?" She came inside. "Did *you* get enough sleep?"

"Maybe a bit of a hangover. I think I had more last night than I realized."

"Everyone but Peter and Sisley did. Are you going to be all right working?"

He huffed something that, had he been in a better mood, might've been a chuckle. "Yes. Obviously."

Amelie raised her eyebrows. She couldn't stand it when he was like that. "No need to be curt. It's not my fault things aren't..." *Going your way*. She managed to swallow the words before they left her lips.

Only a week ago, Bennett had been happy, excited about his new house and his future in Bay Harbor. And then, Amelie surmised, he'd had a heart-to-heart moment with Sisley. Clearly, it hadn't gone well. If he'd come for advice, she'd have told him to ask the girl before buying the house.

"Can I make you breakfast?" she offered gently.

"No, thank you. I'll just have one of these later." He swiped a cookie and, without another word, bumbled back where he'd come from.

Amelie put a hand on her hip. Maybe she was too hard on him. But that sort of tight-lipped behavior was a little provoking, wasn't it? She narrowed her eyes and called after him. "Are you going to move into your new house soon?"

Only the echo answered her.

"Alrighty then," she murmured. "I suppose it doesn't help that the house is smack in between Mela's and Kimmie's. *Awkward*."

"I heard that," Bennett's voice came glumly from the staircase around the corner.

Amelie giggled guiltily and propped the sunroom door open. When she checked last night, the forecast had predicted a thunderstorm. Weather at the coast was famous for turning on a point like a moody ballerina, but so far, so good. Sunlight streamed into the house, red and golden from the leaves of the big maples outside, and the sky was as blue as the sea where the two kissed at the horizon.

The scent of Bennett's coffee was so inviting Amelie made a cup for herself, and then she sat at the island and pulled out her phone.

The letters didn't matter.

If they did, surely Mela's words wouldn't keep circling in her head and keeping her up at night.

She sipped her hot brew until she was fed up with thinking it over. Thinking wasn't going to move anything forward. She was ready to go with feeling.

Calling Charlie *felt* right. She wanted to do it. Whether or not it opened a kettle of fish.

He'd not been in touch since he left Bay Harbor. Amelie knew it wasn't because he'd forgotten her. Not after buying her a huge house to apologize for leaving her thirty years ago. It was too expensive to forget that quickly.

She pressed his number on her phone.

It rang a couple of times before there was an answer. "Amelie?"

"Charlie!" Her heart drummed as if she was back in high school again, finally daring to speak to her crush. "I just wanted to... Is this a good time?" There were voices in the background.

"Amelie, how good to hear your voice." A woman laughed. "Can I call you back in half an hour? Maybe an hour?"

Suddenly, Amelie felt breathless. "Oh, of course. Of course. I didn't mean to... I'll talk to you later. Bye!"

She dropped the call as if it were a red-hot potato. "Goodness."

Bennett rounded the corner, returning his empty mug. "Why goodness? What happened?"

"Nothing."

Even after a bad night, her detective son wasn't easily fooled. His gaze dropped to the phone. "Who'd you call?"

"Nobody." Amelie sighed. "Well. Your father."

He grunted. "Oh, now it's 'my father,' is it?" Then he sighed as well. "Sorry. I'm... It's the hangover. I didn't mean it."

"It's Sisley, not a hangover," Amelie corrected him. "She said no to whatever it was you offered her. You're...*heartbroken*."

His eyebrows dropped low. "Here I am, trying to be nice, and you are... I'm not *heartbroken*." He looked from her to the phone. "How's Charlie?"

"Good." Amelie tilted her head. "I think."

"Why don't you know?" Bennett's voice softened. "Did he not want to talk?"

"I guess...not? I don't know." She pressed a hand to her cheek, willing it to cool down. "He was busy with the...ranch." They had female cowboys these days. Cowgirls. They were called cowgirls.

Amelie tried not to think about laughing cowgirls. She fanned her face. "It's fine. I just thought I'd say hi, catch up. It doesn't mean he's got to drop everything. And I'm having a hot flash. Don't stare. It's impolite."

"O-kay." Bennett held up his hands.

"Ugh." Amelie crumpled. "Listen to us. How did we get to snapping at each other?"

Bennett dropped his hands. "By being fools who let their guard down. And now we're embarrassed and mad at each other for knowing it."

Amelie smiled. "You're so smart. I love you, sweetheart. Don't be late."

"Right." He pulled back and straightened his shoulders. "Well, I suppose I'll see you tonight? Let's have dinner out on the patio, just the two of us, like we used to in the old house."

"Mom might join us."

"I don't mind if she does," he said generously, and then he came over and pressed a kiss on her cheek. "Never mind Charlie, Mom. We're fine without him. We'll keep doing what we've always done."

"Make it up as we go along?"

"Exactly."

"Footloose and fancy-free?" Amelie asked to be sure. Something was really wrong with Bennett if that's how he saw himself. There was no more organized person than her son.

"Yes, why not." His phone dinged, and he glanced at the screen. "I gotta go, Mom. We have a heavy weight to get off the streets before he does more damage, and there's a new lead. Somebody's called in a tip." He turned to leave.

"Be careful, do you hear me?" she called after him. "Do you want a tray of cookies for the incident room?"

But Bennett was already gone.

Amelie hoped he'd at least caught the bit about being careful.

She got up and poured the rest of her coffee away. There was no reason to behave like a jilted bride just because a woman had laughed in the background.

She should call Mela. Ask whether she could help with the dishes from yesterday. Amelie picked up the phone.

"I don't know if there are any dishes left. Sunny won't let me into the kitchen," Mela answered her question. "She's in a bit of a temper, truth be told. I think..." Her voice dropped to a whisper. "I think she's nervous about Travis. Sunny's very protective of the girls."

"I don't blame her," Amelie said. "I'm protective of the girls too. Did you see Kimmie's face when she went to him last night?"

"I've always said she wasn't over him," Mela announced wisely. "She's never been the same since the divorce. I suppose we'll see what happens now. I only know that if I could get into the kitchen, I'd bake little Pippa some cookies."

"I called Charlie," Amelie said casually. "He didn't have time to talk. And a woman was laughing."

"Oh. Well." Mela inhaled audibly. "That could be for any *number* of reasons, Amelie."

"And obviously it wouldn't matter if...you know," Amelie confirmed. "I still like him, sure. But that's it."

"Yeah..." Mela didn't sound entirely convinced. "Amelie—do you want to take a walk at the beach? The weather is beautiful. I can come over."

"Yes, let's," Amelie latched on gratefully. "Just the two of us for once. I'd like that."

"I'll be there in five. Bye!"

Amelie sat a while longer, looking at the stacks of cookies she'd baked because there was a grieving four-year-old in Bay Harbor and because, for a long night, she'd missed Charlie more than she could admit. Then the five minutes were over, and Mela opened the door and called out to wear sandals because the sand was warm enough to walk barefoot.

"I don't know where they are; I'll have to look in the garage. Come in here! Have a cookie!" Amelie got off her chair to find the flip-flops.

"Hi!" Mela poked her head into the kitchen. A fraction of a second later, Amelie's phone rang.

"Oh." Amelie stared at the phone. Mela came and leaned over her shoulder, checking the name that popped up.

"You should probably take that," Mela said loyally and grabbed a cookie. "I'll be out on the patio. Take your time. I have about a hundred books on my phone. There's never enough time to read."

"Thank you," Amelie mouthed and pressed the key. "Yes?"

"Amelie! I'm sorry about that; I just had to wrap something up."

"No problem at all!" Amelie laughed, too bright and cheerful. She cleared her throat and waited until Mela had tiptoed into the sunroom, closing the door behind her.

"Did something happen?"

"Oh. No. I didn't have a reason to call," Amelie admitted sheepishly. "Only the house was so beautiful this morning, and we hadn't talked in a while, so...I just wanted to say hi. I hope I didn't interrupt anything. Um. How are you?"

He laughed. "I'm glad you finally called! I didn't want to be the first, in case...you know, I wondered whether I was too overbearing making you accept the house. I thought maybe I'd scared you off."

"Oh. No. No, I'm not scared. Huh." Amelie pinched her mouth shut; she sounded like a giddy teenager. No. Worse. She sounded like a—

"So I was in a business meeting just now, and we were closing a deal," he interrupted her unhelpful thoughts.

"I thought you had a ranch." Amelie missed the days of long, curly phone cords to twist around your fingers. She picked up a fork, looked at it, and put it down again.

"A ranch is a business," Charlie replied mildly. "I'm running it from Sydney, remember?"

There were no cowgirls in the city, were there? But business was business, not private. Not that there was a reason he shouldn't have private business—

"Amelie? Uh...how are you? Tell me." He cleared his throat. "I've been thinking a lot about Bay Harbor. How is the house? Do you still like it?"

"Oh. The house is wonderful, Charlie," she said. "It's gorgeous. I wish you could see it now that we're all moved in."

"You could give me a tour via phone," he suggested. "We could Facetime."

"I have an Android...and anyway, how are *you*?" Amelie put a hand to her forehead. She'd spent the night *baking*, for crying out loud. She needed a shower, do her hair. Why'd she called when she wasn't—

"I'm good. I had a lot of work waiting for me when I came back, and I..."

"Charlie, about the letters..." she interrupted him, noticing too late that he was still talking.

"Yes?"

"I haven't found them. Mom gave me Dad's boxes, and I haven't found them." She inhaled.

Static crackled in the line as if Charlie was moving. "I'm so sorry. I swear I..."

"No. It doesn't matter." How had Mela phrased it? Amelie couldn't think. Mela had said it so well. "It doesn't matter. I don't want to see them anymore."

The tone of his voice dropped. "I promise I sent them, Amelie. Every single one. I—"

"No, I mean I believe you," Amelie interrupted him. "What I mean to say is that I don't need to find the letters because I *believe* you."

There was a pause before he spoke. "You *believe* me?"

"Yes. I'm sorry, I'm bungling this up." She inhaled weakly. "Um—Mela just came over when you called and—"

"Oh. I'm sorry I called back at a bad time. I didn't realize, you said to—"

"Technically, *you* said—oh, stop. Stop." The kitchen had cooled down, but Amelie felt hot with embarrassment. Here she was, a trained therapist who helped people communicate with each other. She could do better than this. "I meant to say, Charlie, that I miss you. I'm thinking of you, and I thought I should let you know I do believe you sent the letters. Dad must've thrown them away. He had no reason to keep them, after all."

"Oh."

"That was all. I'm sorry if my call interrupted your business... Oh goodness, I even forgot about the time difference. What is it, the middle of the night?" Now that she'd gotten out what she meant to say, thinking was easier.

"It's ten in the evening," he replied. "But that doesn't matter. Thank you. Thank you for calling and telling me." He inhaled. "When I didn't hear from you, I was afraid I'd misread you."

"You misread me? What do you mean?"

"It doesn't matter. It doesn't make a difference now."

Amelie frowned. She didn't make a difference. Maybe she'd read him wrong too. Maybe *she'd* misinterpreted his generosity, the warmth in his eyes, the embrace he'd given his son. "Okay," she said when she could. "I'm sorry."

"Why are you...ah, wait." He chuckled softly, and she couldn't tell whether it was out of nerves or amusement. "Good thing we didn't have email and cell phones back then, Amelie. We'd have talked sideways at each other all the time."

"I'm confused."

"What *I* mean to say is that I miss you too, Amelie."

"You do?"

"I miss Bennett."

Oh—that sort of missing. "Yes."

He exhaled a tense breath. "I sold the ranch."

What did that mean? Was it good or bad? "Oh. Um...congratulations?"

"So I can move back to Bay Harbor," he added.

"You're moving back here? Back to Bay Harbor?" Amelie's phone slipped from her grip and clattered on the counter. She hastily picked it up again.

He didn't seem to have noticed the glitch. "—to grow old in Maine. Going back has changed me. I have missed Bay Harbor every day since I returned, and I realized I spent my life waiting to go back."

"Really?"

"I haven't told anyone yet. I'm not sure what Peter will say. And you." He cleared his throat. "Especially you, Amelie."

"You're coming back."

He waited a moment. "What do you say?"

"You can come back," she said mechanically.

"Yes, but do you *want* me to come back?"

"Yes. Charlie, I do. Of course I do. You're Bennett's dad. It'd be great if you two had a relationship."

"I think so too. Amelie—what about our relationship? There's never been anyone else for me, so I might as well ask now. How do you feel about giving me a second chance?"

Amelie closed her eyes. “I would like that, Charlie,” she whispered when she could. “I think I would like that.”

CHAPTER 12

"Everybody strapped in?" Kimmie asked. "You all have enough space back there?"

"Yep. All good back here." Sisley pulled her seatbelt tight. She was sitting in the back of Travis's rental car. On her left was the baby seat with Lovie inside. Lovie was babbling contentedly to herself, her hands swatting at a rubber giraffe and a silver bell dangling from the seat handle.

On Sisley's right, Pippa was strapped into a forward-facing car seat. The little girl had been glued to Travis's side so far, and Sisley had barely heard a word out of her in the few days they'd shared a house.

"Pippa was looking out of the window but turned her head when she felt Sisley's eyes on her.

"Hi," Sisley said. "How are you, Pippa?"

The eyes blinked. "Good," Pippa said. It was just one word, but it came out loud and clear.

Sisley smiled. "Good. What did you have for breakfast?"

Pippa turned back to the window.

"She had cereal," Travis replied for his daughter. He pulled out of the driveway onto Seasweet and drove toward Main Street.

"It's not important what I ate," Pippa said, as loud and clear as before.

Travis looked at Sisley in the rearview mirror. She nodded that she had this. At least Pippa was talking at all.

"I suppose it isn't," she agreed. "I was just trying to find something to talk about."

"Why?" Pippa was giving Sisley her very undivided attention, the blue eyes like headlamps.

"Because I'd like to get to know you."

"You know me." She spread her arm as if it was self-evident. "I'm Pippa."

"I know your name, but I don't know you as a person," Sisley explained.

"You mean friends," Pippa decided.

Sisley nodded. "Yeah. I would like to know you like a friend."

Pippa turned back to the window, but a little hand reached over the arm of the seat, the fingers wiggling an invitation.

Sisley took it.

"Turn right at the light." Kimmie glanced at her phone. "That's the shortest way to Beach Cove."

Travis turned. "Looks like we're going uphill. Is this the cliff?"

"It will be soon. I've never taken this route," Kimmie said. "I figured it'd be slow, with lots of tourists taking the scenic route. Obviously that was before I knew how few visitors come to Bay Harbor."

"Beach Cove gets much busier than Bay Harbor," Sisley said. "It's got all those cute stores and cafés. And their beaches are great."

"I still don't understand," Travis protested. "Bay Harbor also has cute stores, and the beaches are beautiful. And *empty*. Where can you find empty beaches anymore?"

They'd told him about the empty motel since he arrived. They'd had dinner together. Travis had explained to the family what had happened and asked to be forgiven for the way he handled his and Kimmie's divorce.

Mom was still cautious about him, and Sisley knew it was because she was protective of Kimmie, who clearly was again—still?—head over heels for her ex. But while Mom wasn't as cozy with Travis as she'd been when he and Kimmie had been married, she admitted that he and his little girl needed healing and that there was no better place than Bay Harbor for that.

Travis looked at her in the rearview mirror. "Honest question, Sis. Where else can people find empty beaches like ours?"

"Nowhere as far as I know." Sisley suppressed a smile at Travis's inclusive wording. "Theoretically, our empty beaches should be a big draw for tourists. All these stressed folks from Boston and Connecticut and New York should be *streaming* into Bay Harbor." Lovie burst a spit bubble, and Sisley wiped the baby's chin with a bib.

"Will you look at that," Travis said after a while. "What unbelievable beauty."

They had reached the top of the cliff, and the cove shimmered below, reflecting the brilliant reds and yellows of the foliage on the cliff like a bejeweled mirror. Travis pulled to the side and stopped, and they rolled down the windows, listening to the screams of gulls that chased the salty breeze.

"Beautiful," Sisley agreed and breathed in the marine scents of dried kelp and driftwood, beach grass, and cliff walks. "I can't believe I get to live here."

"The cove is formed by those outcroppings." Kimmie pointed to where the cliff jutted out in a steep, cragged wall. Another cliff did the same from the far side, leaving only a narrow gate between cove and Atlantic. Even though the open ocean crashed white-crested waves against the gate in wild fury at being kept out, what water was channeled into the cove lapped tame and content at the sugar-sand beaches.

"We should get there pretty soon," Sisley murmured. "The drive went by faster than I thought."

"No wonder with this view. I'm not even in a hurry to arrive," Travis replied. "What a gorgeous drive." He started the engine again.

"My phone lost service," Kimmie remarked when they passed the cliffs that formed the cove. She shook it as if that would make the GPS connect again, then slipped it in the door pocket. "At least there's nothing much to navigate. That's the town down there."

For a while, they lost view of the ocean as the road led through swelling meadows on one side and deep blueberry forest on the other. "Who owns this land?" Travis asked. "This must be worth millions. The view on the other side of that hill is even better than at the vista point where we stopped. You should be able to see the entire cove, including the town."

"I have no idea. I've never taken this road either." Sisley leaned over the baby to see better. Pippa was still holding her hand, but she'd been quiet since asking for a drink fifteen minutes earlier. "I do hope the lucky owner isn't a real estate developer. This is too beautiful to build on."

"Maybe it's public land," Travis said. "Though if I were to pay taxes for this, I'd at least want a hiking path over that hill."

"Turn toward the sea next time you can," Kimmie said. "We should be almost there. There's a public parking lot by the harbor."

They drove down the cliff and glimpsed the sea again. Then the bright little town opened its arms and streets in an easy welcome, and they soon found the harbor, where they parked and got out.

Sisley grabbed her diaper backpack and knotted the baby sling across her chest. She giggled because Lovie had figured out how to make a new grunting sound and was listening to herself with an expression of wonder.

"Hmmm," Kimmie said and inhaled deeply. "Smells good! What do you all say to lunch before we go on? I know we had a massive breakfast, but I'm hungry."

"I'm hungry too," Pippa announced. She'd unceremoniously dropped Sisley's hand as soon as they arrived and stood by her father with a no-nonsense expression on her face.

"Well then, I suppose we should eat," Sisley said and put Lovie into the sling. The baby grunted but then got busy snuggling up to her. Sisley hugged her tighter. "I should nurse this one, too. She gets fussy when she's hungry, and once she starts, she might not stop even when she's full."

"I like the baby," Pippa said approvingly.

"She's very relatable," Sisley replied and pulled the fabric over Lovie's head so she wouldn't get sunburnt, leaving only a small slit for the eyes. The baby loved peeking at the world from her marsupial pouch.

"Look, that's what smells good." Kimmie pointed at a small restaurant by the water. "The Harbor Shack."

They went inside and were seated by a lady in her fifties, who introduced herself as Sharon as she led the way to a booth. The place was mostly empty, but there was a young couple, a sporty blonde and her beau, who looked like they were ditching high school for a milkshake.

Sharon stuffed her blank notepad back into the pocket of her tight jeans. "I'll bring your drinks in a whiff. Have a look at the menus."

"I'll take the flounder," Sisley decided after studying the laminated card. The savory aromas filling the air already made her mouth water. "I don't know if I've ever had flounder."

Sharon returned with Pippa's Fanta and everyone else's iced teas in time to catch the words. "The flounder is good," she confirmed. "My friend won't order anything else, and she's lived in Beach Cove forever. Her ancestor was a witch and basically founded the town. Well—truth be told, she's a bit stubborn. My friend, not the founding witch. The other dishes are very good too."

Sisley turned so Sharon wouldn't see her smile at her rambling and ordered the flounder. They also ordered coconut shrimp to share, fried clam platters and lobster rolls, and a seafood quesadilla with fries and slaw for Pippa.

"I've never heard of that combo," Kimmie remarked when they were alone. "But I think it'll taste great, Pippa."

"I'd better take care of Lovie before the food comes." Sisley went to ask Sharon for a quiet spot to nurse and change Lovie, and Sharon showed her to an airy office with a table and a rocking chair and sweetly supplied milk and cookies, and a trash bag. Clearly, the woman had grandbabies.

"So what should we do after we eat?" Travis asked after Sisley returned. "Do you want us to come to the candy store with you, Sisley? We'll do whatever you think is best."

"I'll just go by myself for starters, I think."

Kimmie raised an eyebrow. "I'm not happy about the phones not working here."

"Honestly, my worst-case scenario is buying salty instead of sweet licorice." Really, Sisley wanted Kimmie and Travis to have some time together. They were always surrounded by Kimmie's friends and family in Bay Harbor. An hour or so alone was just the thing for them.

"I want to come to the candy store," Pippa said suddenly. "Can I? Please?"

Sisley nodded. "Yes, that's a good idea. I'll take Lovie and Pippa to the store with me." She patted her sister's hand. "We'll get candy apples and take a little stroll through town, and then we'll meet up again."

"You want to take both Lovie and Pippa?" Travis looked unsure.

"Of course." Sisley smiled at him. "We'll have the best time, won't we, Pippa?"

"I don't know," the little girl responded doubtfully. "But I want a candy apple."

Kimmie swallowed a laugh, and Sisley chuckled. "We'll get you one, and let's hope the rest will be fun too. We can go window shopping."

Now that Pippa had started talking, she kept going, and the exploration of the topic of window shopping—what was it, *why* was it, and was it really better than riding one's tricycle—took them most of the way through a delicious lunch. Even Sharon had a few thoughts to share.

Travis insisted on paying. "At least it's nice and empty now," Sharon said as she ran his card. "There were so many tourists this summer. We earned a golden nose, but I thought the town would burst." She shook her head, looking put upon. "I'd rather stay poor and get home in time to see the grandkids. You know what I mean?"

"We could use some of your visitors in Bay Harbor," Kimmie said and stood. "I don't know why it is so crowded over here and virtually empty in our town. It's not even an hour away. Less over the cliff."

"We have buses shuttling people in from Sandville and Bay Port. That helps, especially when there's nowhere for folks to stay the night," Sharon said. "And if I remember right, there are just not enough restaurants in Bay Harbor. People have to eat. Summer is crazy for the Shack."

"Actually, there's a motel in Bay Harbor," Sisley mentioned on the way to the door.

"But it's run down and depressing," Sharon said. "Isn't it?"

"It was just renovated." Sisley stopped by the hostess table. "Here, have a look." She pulled up a few pictures of the motel in its new glory on her phone.

"Oh. Wow." Sharon flipped through the album. "I wouldn't mind staying there myself. Who knew?" She handed the phone back.

"If anyone asks, please recommend the motel," Sisley said. "It's on the brink of bankruptcy. The owner is the kindest person in the world, and the motel means the world to him. His grandpa built it after he had a dream that he should provide a place for lost souls. But we need paying tourists to pitch in." She smiled.

"Do you have cards?" Sharon asked. "We have a small inn in town, but it's got a waitlist fifteen feet long. They sure wouldn't mind having another place to recommend."

Sisley beamed. "I do have cards!" She pulled a stack from her diaper bag. Peter had asked them to hand out as many as they could.

Sharon took them and divided the stack in half, putting one on the hostess stand beside the register. "Claire?" she said, turning to the sporty blonde who was laughing with her boyfriend. "If you ask your mom to give these to Maisie, I won't tell her you're ditching PE."

Unfazed at the threat, the girl unfolded lithely from her booth and came forward. "Sure." Claire took the cards. "They've booked British weirdos through the winter and have to turn people away every day." On the table behind her, her young man stood and started stacking the dishes as if he was employed by the restaurant. "It looks nice. Maybe I'll come to stay myself sometime. Bring some friends, you know?" Claire gave them a bright smile. "In Beach Cove, everyone knows everyone else."

"I don't know if that's a bad thing when it comes to you, missy," the waitress muttered and checked her phone. "You have math next. Off you go. I'll check with your teacher that you showed your face."

"No, you won't." Claire's eyes were laughing.

"Yes, I absolutely will. I'm playing Monopoly with her tonight."

"Fine. Tell Kevin I said bye." Claire leaned in and kissed Sharon's cheek, then waved and left, tucking the cards in the back pocket of her jeans.

"Takes a *village*," the waitress complained, but her hand went to her cheek where the girl had kissed her.

"What village?" Pippa had followed the exchange with much interest.

"It means all the people in town have to help raise a child," Travis explained and took her hand.

"Like me?" Pippa looked up. "Because Mum is in heaven and can't do it herself anymore?"

Sisley took the girl's other hand. "All kids need to be raised by a village," she said. "Because all kids need a lot of different people. Don't you think?"

Pippa thought for a moment, and then she nodded. "I guess so." She let go of her dad, her face a little brighter.

Travis threw Sisley a grateful look, and she thought once again that the most important thing was to not feel alone. For her, for Lovie, for Pippa. Even for hard-boiled eggs like Kimmie and Travis.

"Let's go get that candy apple dessert." She squeezed Pippa's hand.

They thanked Sharon and left, filled with delicious food and the kindness of strangers.

"We'll see you in an hour!" Sisley waved cheerfully at her companions.

"Wait—at least take the car keys," Kimmie said and held them up. "In case you need something for the kids.

There are snacks and water in the trunk, and spare leggings..."

"In case I pee," Pippa explained.

"I hear you." Sisley laughed and caught the keys, and then she took off before her sister could change her mind and decided to play safety guard after all.

The photo of her uncle was tucked safely in the pocket of her diaper bag.

CHAPTER 13

A dam had been broken, a barrier removed. Now that she had decided to trust Sisley, Pippa talked and talked. Sisley listened and did her best to field the questions that rolled her way like an avalanche of curiosity. From her pouch, Lovie listened, squirming now and then to see the older girl.

"Look, Pippa," Sisley said after walking up a steep, narrow street marked Marina Alley. They'd been wandering the quaint cobblestone streets for a half hour, pausing often to get in some proper window shopping as per Pippa's request. "That must be the Candy Apple Store." She pointed at the cheerful red awning.

"Yay!"

Sisley threw a glance at the bookstore that was opposite the candy store. The window was crammed full of old and antique books. They seemed to call her name as loud and clear as if they had voices. She wanted to go in badly, but with two little ones, it wasn't a good idea.

"Shall we go in?" Sisley squared her shoulders.

"Yes?" said Pippa, and when Sisley looked at her, she saw the little girl was watching her. "Do you want to go in that store for..." She tilted her head, considering the old books. "Boring books?"

"How do they know they're boring?"

"Mum stood the TV on old books because they were boring."

"Oh. Well, maybe that was just *those* books," Sisley said. "Every book is different, you know. Some are exciting."

"Like TV?"

Sisley scratched her chin. "Kind of. You know what, let's go get our candy. I can always come back to look at the books."

"You could try and find the exciting ones," Pippa encouraged the plan.

"Exactly." Sisley led her across the street and pushed against the glossy red door. It opened easily.

"Ooh," Pippa said and went inside. "Gosh. Sisley, look!"

Sisley followed her, letting the door fall shut behind them. "How pretty!"

The store was a child's dream. Sunlight streamed through the large shop windows that looked over the roofs leading down to the sea and reflected sweet and golden as honey off the wooden floorboards. There was a long glass shelf in the center of the room, and even longer tables full of pretty glass containers in all shapes ran down the sides. On the walls hung cheerful vintage posters of candies and ice creams, cakes, and cream tortes. But the biggest pop of color came from the candy. It looked as if a rainbow was bottled in the glass containers, inviting kids and adults alike to touch and try. Buttery striped candies, delicate cream swirls and crackle pop, chocolate chunks studded with walnuts and toffee crunch, saltwater taffy to melt in the mouth, candy buttons on paper, thick rolls of licorice, truffles, and lollipops shaped like butterflies and frogs and bumblebees, bags bursting with kettle corn.

"Oh my goodness," said Sisley, letting her eyes wander over the treasures, and "Oh my goodness," whispered Pippa after her.

Someone chuckled, and Sisley looked up.

"Come on in," an old man said. His clothes hung from his wizened frame, and his voice creaked with age like a pirate ship, but he nodded kindly. He limped from the back to the counter. Like the rest of the store, it was made of glass and golden wood. "Have a look around and sample all you like from the trays. I'm about to close the store for the winter, so you might as well eat all you can."

"Yeeess," Pippa said and reached for the nearest tray, letting her hand hover over it while her round eyes waited for Sisley's permission.

Sisley nodded. "Only from the trays," she reminded the little girl. "Once you find something you like, we'll buy some from inside the container."

Pippa picked a piece of marshmallow the color of toasted hazelnut and carefully put it in her mouth. "Hmmm," she hummed happily. "Do you want one, Sisley?"

Sisley also took a piece. "Delicious. Let's get some for us and some more for the people at home, okay?"

Pippa nodded enthusiastically. "Our village really wants marshmallows," she declared. "Can I bring them some?"

"That's a good idea. I'm sure the village would enjoy it." Sisley scooped a small bag, then pointed to another sample. "Let's try the taffy," she said. "It says on the label that they make it themselves in the store." She handed Pippa a pretty cube.

"I make candy apples too," the owner said. He was smiling as if he enjoyed watching them. "The store is empty, so I can make them to order."

"What sort of candy apples do you have?" Sisley guided Pippa to the counter. She'd been worried the child would go haywire, surrounded by temptations. But now that Sisley saw how politely Pippa helped herself to only one piece from each tray, she realized her apprehension had been unfounded. She let go of Pippa's hand, and the girl smiled up at her.

Sisley smiled back. Young as Pippa was, she was perceptive. She understood Sisley trusted her to behave herself now, and she both acknowledged the trust and promised to keep it. Sisley nodded, and Pippa went to a display of cotton candy to pick a sugary wisp off the sampler.

"Nice kid," the owner said in a low voice. His heavy lids drooped lower as he squinted at Sisley. "Do I know you by any chance? Did you come here last summer?"

"I've never been in here before." She slid the diaper bag off her shoulder and set it on the counter. She wasn't sure how to segue from candy and kids to the photo of Uncle Finn. "Do you have red candy apples?"

"I have all sorts of candy apples," the owner answered. "Red is always a winner. But I also make chocolate ones, with any topping you like. My rocky road bestseller has dark chocolate and marshmallows and nuts and salty pretzel bits." He glanced at the sparkling steel drum beside him. "I can make caramel too. It takes a bit more time if you want to get the best consistency. Not too soft and not too chewy. You want both caramel and apple in each bite." He looked at her expectantly.

"I'll take three apples with red glaze," Sisley decided. Mom, Peter, and Sunny would like the classic of their childhood. "And two rocky road, please." Amelie and Bennett were the perfect candidates for those. Especially Bennett. He could use something extra sweet and crunchy now that he had that stressful case on his hands.

"Coming right up. It'll take a few minutes, but you can leave and come back if you like. I'm open until...let's say five. I usually close at four, but I'll stay open for you."

"Aww. No need. I don't think Pippa exactly minds waiting."

"They usually don't." The old man chuckled, and then he patted the counter and turned to make the apples.

The door opened with the clinging of a silver bell, and a tall woman around fifty came in, carrying a two-year-old. The woman was very pale with platinum-white hair that looked natural, and her bright blue eyes went straight to Sisley. "Hello," the woman said and hitched her granddaughter higher. The little girl was exceptionally pretty. The two made a striking pair.

"Hello," Sisley said, trying not to stare. "Pippa. Come over here."

"No worries," the woman said. "A red apple, please, Martin."

Martin looked up, blinking at the woman. "Coming up right after this lady gets hers, Sam. Red, did you say? Is Brandie in town?"

"Yes, and she is."

"I'll bring the apple over to the bookstore," he promised.

"Nah, I'll wait." Sam fished a salt licorice coin off a tray and popped it into her mouth. "The books and I are *done* with each other." She looked at Sisley. "Um. For the day, I mean."

"Oh, is that beautiful bookstore across the street yours?" Sisley went to steer Pippa away from a tray she'd almost emptied. Cheeks stuffed with taffy, Pippa looked at the little girl and waved. The little girl waved back. Pippa grabbed Sisley's hand and leaned against her leg, staring wordlessly at the newcomers.

"Ye-es, it is," Sam said doubtfully. "Are you on vacation?"

"I live in Bay Harbor," Sisley said. "We heard about the store and came to sample the candy." She smiled an apology for the almost-empty samplers. In all politeness, Pippa had abandoned her one-piece policy after all.

"Bay Harbor," Sam said. "It's not that far, isn't it?"

"Half an hour." Sisley nodded. "We took a beautiful road across the cliff."

"Ye-es," Sam said again, sounding even more doubtful now. "It's a pretty drive, but that street sees a lot of flooding in summer and snow and ice in the winter. I got stuck up there myself once. People have mostly stopped using it."

"Because it's *haunted*," Martin threw in.

"No, of course it's not haunted." Sam threw him a look back. "Don't spook your guests."

"I didn't realize it floods and freezes so often. That's too bad." Sisley smiled. "We could use some of Beach Cove's overflowing tourism over there to revive things. I love a sleepy little town, but our small businesses are hurting."

"I hear you." Sam set her pretty granddaughter down and adjusted the shoulder strap of her slouchy bag. "We had a summer not so long ago where the tourists didn't come, and it was a disaster. Well..." She narrowed her eyes as if she was thinking. "Well, things have changed. Maybe that street isn't as bad as it used to be, and people will rediscover it."

"That would be great." Sisley thought the conversation a little strange. Had the weather pattern changed that much?

The owner had heated the red glaze and dipped the apples, and they were drip-cooling on wax paper while he melted chocolate and chopped nuts on a wooden board. The rich, sweet scents were as tempting to Sisley as sirens to a sailor. "I just had an entire platter of crispy flounder...but this smells too good." Sisley fished a chocolate pretzel from a tray. Pippa followed her example.

The golden-haired granddaughter held out a hand. Her eyes were like green spotlights on Pippa, who handed over her pretzel and took a new one.

"You wouldn't happen to have an interest in play dates, would you?" Sam was watching the kids too. "Little Brooke here doesn't have many kids to play with, only a couple of twin babies." She smiled fondly as if she was close to the twins. "But they're too young to play with Brooke. Maybe they would be good company for whoever lives in that sling, though." She nodded at Lovie, who was watching from the safety of her pouch.

"Actually, that would be great," Sisley said. "Pippa would probably enjoy having a friend. And I'd love to find other babies for Lovie."

"I think they would get along very well," Sam said. "I have a good feeling about this."

"Me too," Sisley agreed. "Only Pippa isn't my daughter. I'm not sure how long she'll be in Bay Harbor."

"Long," Pippa said and held out a hand. Brooke took it. "Do you want to try jellybeans?" Pippa asked solicitously and pulled Brooke with her, away from the adults.

"Oh, I don't know about that," Sisley said. "Um. Pippa?"

Sam shook her head. "They're fine," she promised. "Brooke is very level-headed. For a two-year-old, I mean."

Sisley laughed. How level-headed could a two-year-old possibly be? "I'll pay for whatever they eat," she told the storekeeper.

He waved the remark away. "No worries," he murmured, his old hands expertly coating the apples with roasted nuts.

Sisley took a pencil and a piece of scrap paper from a bowl by the register and scribbled on it. "Here's my number," she said and handed it to Sam. "And email—in case the phone doesn't work. Of course I'll have to ask Pippa's dad about the playdate too."

"Thank you." Sam tucked the note away. "I'll be in touch. I'm always looking for ways to socialize that kid."

The shopkeeper huffed a laugh, and Sam squared her shoulders.

"By the way," Sisley turned to him. Most of the apples were done and waiting for the candy shell to dry and harden. "I found this old photo in my grandmother's things, and I was wondering whether you knew who this is. It says Finn Sullivan on the back, and a friend told me you're a Sullivan too." She opened the diaper bag.

"Finn Sullivan?" Martin put the last apple on the wax paper and wiped his hands, then picked half-glasses from a ledge under the counter and put them on his nose. “Finn?”

“Martin,” Sam said softly.

Sisley showed him the photo of Mom’s uncle in his swim trunks and decorated with seaweed. “Do you know him?”

“Of course.” The old man tilted the photo into the light. “That’s my Finn. He’s my son.”

“He’s your *son*,” Sisley repeated. “That’s...a surprise. Um. I don’t understand.” How could Julie’s brother be the shopkeeper’s son?

Sam stepped closer, and Martin showed her the photo. “That’s Smuggler’s Beach,” Sam said. “Isn’t it? Look at that rock.” She pointed.

The shopkeeper nodded. “He often went swimming there.”

“Smuggler’s Beach?” Sisley repeated slowly, feeling stupid. She still couldn’t put Martin and Finn and Julie together in her head. What had Constance been up to?

“The story goes that in the olden days, a pirate captain used the cliff caves to tuck away smuggled goods. Who knows if it’s true?” Martin laid the photo down, his eyes glued to his son’s face. “You can only see the caves at low tide. I never thought it was a good place to hide anything. Come high tide, it all washes right back out.”

“The town closed the beach in the early nineties. The tourists would forever get in trouble checking out the caves and getting trapped by the tide coming in. Our fishermen couldn’t keep up saving them.” Sam shook her head, exasperated either over the tourists' naivete or the closing of a favorite beach, or maybe, the fishermen.

The shopkeeper pointed a trembling finger at the photo. "Do you know where Finn is?"

CHAPTER 14

"I'm so sorry. I don't know where he is." Sisley gulped a breath of air. She hadn't expected to stumble across Finn's *dad.* Had nobody told Martin what had happened?

The light in the shopkeeper's eyes dimmed. "Do you know anything about him?"

She hesitated but then softly said, "They say he and his sister had a boating accident."

"Hmm."

"Martin." Sam sounded alarmed. "Look. She's not feeling well."

Sisley turned to her, dazed. It was true. All of a sudden, she wasn't feeling well. She felt dizzy and would have liked to sit down.

"These are done." Slow and deliberate, Martin wrapped the apples in cellophane and placed them in small paper bags. Then he turned back to Sisley and smiled, sad and kind. "They're on the house if I can keep the photo."

Sisley inhaled. "My grandmother's name was Julie Palmer." She slid the photo closer to him. A father's claim overrode that of a niece, and she'd already taken photographs of both the face and the name on the back for Mom.

"Julie Palmer. I haven't heard that name in a long time." The man rubbed a veined hand over his forehead. "Oh, dear."

"Yeah," Sam said as if she'd seen this coming. "You both look like you should sit down."

Sisley blinked at the pale woman. As far as she could tell, Sam had nothing to do with either Finn or Julie. But she couldn't be sure, and she liked the older woman. It'd be good to have her there when she talked to Martin. Last but not least because— "Pippa?" Sisley turned.

"They're under the toffee table," Sam told her. "They're having a conversation."

Supporting the baby in her sling, Sisley bent to look under the table. Sam's blond granddaughter was whispering, and Pippa listened intently.

"Can she talk?" Sisley asked, surprised. Of course she'd read up on developmental stages while pregnant, and she'd been under the impression that Baby Brooke should only be able to string a few words together—not tell entire stories. But maybe the little girl was older than she looked. Sometimes it was hard to tell.

"She's sort of precocious." Sam raised an eyebrow that was more worried than proud. "She didn't say a single word for two years, and we were all starting to freak out. Then one day a few weeks ago, she asked for more milk. Just like that, in a complete sentence including please and thank you. I almost fell off my chair." She shrugged as if little Brooke had her stumped.

"Maybe she's gifted."

"Probably," Sam said darkly.

Sisley turned back to the shopkeeper, who'd finished Sam's apple as well and was again studying the photo with a wistful smile. "Do you have time to talk?" she asked. "Is there a place where we could sit?"

"Sam? Where should we go?"

"Marketplace Café," Sam said immediately. "I'm dying for a coffee. Oh—that is, if you two want me there?"

"Yes," both Martin and Sisley said in unison, and then all three of them had to laugh a little. It cheered up the atmosphere.

"I'll entertain the kids so you two can talk," Sam promised.

Martin closed the store while Sisley and Sam extracted the kids from the toffee table. The café was a short walk away. Progress was slow because Pippa refused to let go of Brooke's hand, and Brooke, however advanced her vocabulary, was still very much a toddler and more interested in the beetles crawling on the sideway than brisk walks. Martin, leaning heavily on Sam's arm, said it didn't matter since he couldn't go any faster anyway, and as far as he was concerned, the town needed more toddlers and beetles altogether. Sisley made up the rear of the small group, taking the ample opportunity to text Kimmie where she was and what she'd found out so far.

Will meet you there, Kimmie texted back immediately. *Good coffee. Don't ask for too much cake. 1 slice per person rule.*

Everything about Beach Cove was a smidge peculiar, Sisley thought. The people, the toddlers, even the cafés. Something growled faintly as if disagreeing with her thoughts from far away. She glanced at the sky. The predicted thunderstorm had started to scraggle ashen lines into the azure sky.

But it was still sunny, and when they finally traversed the marketplace and reached the café, there were only a couple of empty bistro tables left outside. Sisley gratefully lowered herself into a chair. A sliver of sea was visible beyond the marketplace fountain.

A young man in light-up sneakers came over. "Raspberry roll is out. We still have lemon and carrot."

"Lemonade and lemon cream cake, Mikey," Sam said and looked at Sisley. "Unless you want coffee and carrot cake? Those are the options today. Raspberry is best, but it never lasts long."

"Em made extra because of the lobster fishers," Mikey said as if that explained anything. "But when they found out, they also ate extra."

"Um. Lemonade and lemon cream cake, please," Sisley said politely. "I'll share a piece with Pippa." Travis would already tell her off for stuffing the girl with sugary treats.

"Great." Mikey looked relieved. "Pretty sure we have three slices left." He hurried off before they could order more.

"So." Martin had caught his breath. "I think we should introduce ourselves properly since we haven't yet. I'm Martin Sullivan."

"I'm Sam Bowers," Sam said. "Owner of the local antique books store and grandmother to little Brooke."

"Very nice to meet you." Sisley folded her hands. "I'm Sisley Beckett. I just moved to Bay Harbor, but my mother lived there as a child. Julie Palmer was my grandmother."

"Do you know where Julie is?" Martin followed Sisley's example and folded his hands. His fingers still trembled. Whether it was nerves or old age, she didn't know.

"Unfortunately, I never met Julie," Sisley said slowly. She wasn't sure how to proceed.

"Can we play at the fountain?" Pippa asked.

"It's too far away." Sisley squinted at it.

"It's all right with me if it's all right with you," Sam said. "Beach Cove is safe as can be, and we'll be able to see them from here."

"Okay. Go ahead, but make sure to take Brooke's hand and not let go."

"Come on!" Pippa took her new friend's hand, and they toddled off slowly but with confidence.

"You never met Julie because..." Martin raised a questioning eyebrow.

There was no way of sugar coating it. "As far as we know, she and Finn went missing at sea in a boating accident. They were never found," Sisley said.

The lemonade arrived, and she took a thirsty sip. Then she opened the sling. Lovie was getting hot and started to squirm. Squawking baby on lap, she smiled an apology for the constant interruptions. "The thing is...Finn was her *brother*. But...well... If you're his father, that doesn't seem quite right anymore."

Martin closed his eyes and leaned back into his chair.

After a few seconds that seemed like minutes, Sisley looked to Sam for help.

"Martin," Sam said gently and put a pale hand on his weathered one. "Tell her, huh? It doesn't matter now."

He opened his eyes. There was a faraway look in them now as if his mind had wandered back in years and time to a different life. "Julie and Finn were not brother and sister," he said in his deep, creaking-ship voice. "They were star-crossed lovers."

"But are you sure?" Lovie wailed, and Sisley put her on her chest, cradling the baby's fuzzy head in her hand and patting her back with the other. Unexpected as it was, she couldn't argue against Martin's claim, knowing as little about Finn as she did.

Sam nodded a confirmation. "It was their secret."

"I don't think Mom knows this," Sisley said weakly.

"Who is Mom?" Martin's eyes sharpened.

"Pamela Beckett. Julie's daughter."

"Ah." Martin blinked a few times, his lids heavy. "Little Mela. She disappeared too, after the kids went missing. Now she's come back to Bay Harbor, has she?"

"Mom was always told Julie and Finn were siblings." Sisley suddenly felt like she was poking her nose into things she wasn't supposed to know. "Though...it's true that she doesn't know much about Uncle Finn."

"Yes, I can imagine." Martin shook his head. "Finn was careful he wouldn't be found out."

The lemon cake arrived, and Lovie started to squirm again, trying to lift her head and see what was happening.

"Poor Julie," Sam said quietly. Then she added, "I didn't know her well, of course. I only saw her a couple of times when she visited Finn in Beach Cove. Once I saw her crying as she left the candy store, and it always stuck with me."

"Of course she was crying," Martin said. "It was a terrible arrangement for her."

"Oh." Sisley handed Lovie to Sam as if Sam were family. The older woman took the baby without hesitation, immediately starting to sway in the way of experienced mothers and grandmothers. "My head hurts."

Lost in the past, Martin didn't hear. "And of course Finn's hands were bound."

Sisley took another sip of the icy lemonade, letting it cool her throat. Then she looked up. "What happened?" she asked.

CHAPTER 15

"Finn was married," Martin said. "But not to Julie."

"Oh no," Sisley said.

"It was not a good marriage." Martin's throat moved as if he was trying to swallow the memory back down. "They were too young. But they fell pregnant, so they got married. That's what people did, back then. Didn't work out for all of them, though."

"*They* are Finn and...who?"

"Her name was Melanie." Martin smiled a sad smile. "And after giving birth, she had a terrible, terrible case of the blues."

"It's called postpartum depression," Sam said sternly. "You know the proper term, Martin."

"Aye, I do." He nodded. "Don't change a thing what you call it now, Sam, because back then, nobody knew diddly-squat about how to help it. The doctors told her to calm down and drink more water. Didn't help none, all that water."

"What happened?" Sisley felt bad for asking the old man to dig up painful memories. But she wanted to tell

Mom as much as she could in return for losing her an uncle.

"Melanie wasn't in a state to get along with anyone, let alone Finn. She figured he'd destroyed her life because she sure didn't want that baby." He frowned. "But even though she was spitting mad and couldn't stand the sight of him, she also wasn't about to let him go. She threatened to do all kinds of things if he divorced her." He looked at Sisley.

"Bad things?"

He opened his hands and looked to the sky as if looking for an answer that eluded him. "Finn wanted the baby safe. He did as best he could by Melanie, made sure her mom watched out for her and the baby both. They took what he earned, but they wouldn't give him his daughter. He didn't push for a divorce because he wanted to make sure Kitty was all right. If Melanie ever... Well, he wanted to be next in line to get Kitty. He didn't want her to go to Melanie's family."

"His daughter's name is Kitty?"

He nodded. "She was the light of his life, despite the troubles with her mama."

"How did Finn and Julie meet?"

"I inherited the family's candy store. I'd grown tired of fishing out of Portland anyway, so I packed up and moved back to Beach Cove, and I asked Finn to help me run the store in the summers when it gets busy. He was a teacher, always looking for ways to earn money in the summer when school was out."

"And Julie?"

The old man smiled. "Came into the store some bright day while Finn was making candy apples. I knew right away the two were meant for each other." His face softened. "It was like someone switched on the lights in their eyes. I'd never seen Finn so happy."

Sisley pressed her lips together. There were always two sides to a story, even to Finn and Melanie's. But it was hard to be mad at someone who had loved Julie.

"But they couldn't get married," she said.

"No, they couldn't. But they always told me they didn't care about a piece of paper." He shook his head.

"What did Melanie think about that?" Sisley asked cautiously.

"Well, of course she couldn't know. She allowed Finn to see Kitty for holidays, and she let him send her letters and cards. The judge said he should have more. Melanie said no. Finn didn't want Kitty to deal with Melanie fussing if he insisted. But he also wasn't about to give up what little contact he had."

"Oh no." Sisley couldn't imagine. To be stuck with an abusive partner—at least Lars had made a clean break. After the initial shock, it'd been a huge relief. How would it be if the mother was the abuser and the kid lived with her? If what she heard was true, Sisley couldn't blame Finn for holding on to any contact he had while also trying for the sake of his daughter to placate his wife as best he could.

"So Finn and Julie were careful," Martin concluded. "Melanie was all the way in Portland, but she had an aunt in Beach Cove. Julie came to the candy store once in a while, but there was nothing suspicious about that. Everyone came to the candy store once in a while. And in Bay Harbor, where Julie lived, they claimed to be brother and sister. It was good enough. There wasn't much traffic between the towns."

"Right. Plus, the road was haunted."

"Yep." He nodded. "Finn taught school in Portland and came up here in the summer to help in the store and be with Julie."

"Sounds *awful*," said Sam. "Poor babies."

"I don't recommend it," the old shopkeeper said. He sounded sad.

Sisley cleared her throat. "My mom—Mela—doesn't know who her dad is," she said softly. "It wouldn't be Finn, would it?"

Maybe, under all the wrinkles of age, Martin's forehead crumpled. It was hard to tell. "I would think so," he said quietly. "I knew they loved each other, but I'm ashamed to say that Finn and I didn't see eye to eye over Melanie and Julie and what a man should and shouldn't do. We had a fight, and that year, he stopped working for me. Next I knew, I saw Julie walking up Marina Alley with a baby in her arms. But she, too, wouldn't tell me anything. Only said it was hers, and that was enough." He rubbed a hand over his face. "I was raised different. I was fed up with hippies, and babies, and my son never doing the right thing as I saw it. Now I know better."

"He was doing the best he could," Sam agreed softly.

"He wasn't too smart even though he was a teacher," Martin murmured. "He had too much heart and not enough brains."

"He had plenty of brains," Sam said, a note of impatience in her voice. She wiggled Lovie, who was squeaking joyfully. "It was a different time, Martin. And you were not as nice as you are now."

"I tried." Martin sighed. "Finn would visit sometimes, but as soon as I would ask about Julie, he'd clam up."

"He was probably scared you'd yell at him again," Sam said sourly. "He had enough to deal with and was just trying for a bit of happiness."

"Maybe. He sure was not one for conflict. He and Julie were a right pair of innocent babes. And then..." He folded his hands on his lap. "I sit down to watch the news on the television, and the anchor lady said two people were lost at sea. And when I got over to Beach Cove, the baby was gone too, and they wouldn't tell me who took her because I wasn't a relative." He cleared his throat. "And that was it for my family. I had no one left."

"I'm so sorry. Did you at least get to talk to the police?"

"I sure did. I told them who Finn was, and I asked them to keep it out of the news for Kitty's sake. They looked into Melanie and her family to see if they had anything to do with it, but that all checked out. Melanie had found someone new too, and there were living in Vermont by then. She wasn't interested in keeping track of Finn as long as he sent her money and didn't ask to see his daughter. I sent her a letter saying my son was missing, and I would send the money for Kitty now."

"Oh. My. Goodness." Sisley leaned back. At the same moment, she spotted Kimmie and Travis marching toward the fountain. "My sister is here." She texted Kimmie because it was too far to call for her. Kimmie first looked at her phone and then in her direction. She waved and ambled over to meet them, bringing the kids in tow.

"This is my sister Kimmie and her...friend, Travis." Sisley introduced everyone.

"Do you have a bike?" Kimmie asked suddenly.

"It keeps me young." Martin smiled at her. "Why?"

"I think we met before. Just...passed each other." Kimmie smiled back but didn't say anything else.

Sisley stood. "I'm sorry for running away the minute you join us, Kimmie, but I have to nurse Lovie, or I'll be in trouble."

"There's a rocking chair in the upstairs office." Sam pointed over her shoulder at the café. "It's all set up for nursing. Tom will be inside; he'll show you." She handed Lovie over, who immediately started hungrily rooting around Sisley's neck. "I'll catch up your sister if you like."

"Catch me up, huh?" Travis had pulled empty chairs up to the table, and Kimmie sat. "Go on."

"Brace yourselves." Sisley kissed Lovie and left. The Café's owner, Tom, showed her the rocking chair and closed the door behind him. With a sigh, Sisley sank back into the soft cushions and closed her eyes.

Poor Finn. Poor Julie. Poor old Martin, all alone with his regrets.

And poor *Mom*.

When Lovie was done, Sisley gently patted her back.

She wouldn't call Mom to tell what she'd learned about Finn. She'd sit down with her and tell her everything face to face.

And then, maybe, Mom would meet her grandpa.

For some reason, it only now occurred to Sisley that Martin might be her great-grandpa. Lovie's great-great-grandpa.

"Wow," she whispered.

Startled, Lovie lifted her head to look at her. It barely wobbled with the effort even though it lasted only a second before her head fell back on Sisley.

"Good job." Sisley stroked the downy hair and stood. "Should we go back down?"

"La!" Lovie flailed, and her tiny palm landed on Sisley's mouth with a smack.

Sisley pressed a kiss on it. "I *know*."

Sunny, Martin, even Lovie—their family was growing in crooked ways. But that was okay.

"It's fine," she whispered to Lovie. "Crooked branches make apples as sweet as the straight ones."

She went back downstairs, winding her way through the busy café, when something caught her attention.

Those shoulders, that hair... Sisley stopped. Was that *Bennett*? He was sitting with his back to where she stood, talking intently to a woman across the table.

The woman's eyes were locked on Bennett's, her mouth pursed as if she was silently repeating what he was telling her. He had her undivided attention.

She was older than Bennett, but she was absolutely beautiful.

Not in a conventional way, not by a narrow nose and thin waist and glossy hair. Her beauty was competent and good-humored and smart. She looked like someone who moved mountains to meet after work. Someone who had your back even when you messed up. Someone who was there for your bad jokes as long as you listened to hers.

She had all the beauty of a best friend.

Sisley took a deep breath, almost gasping for breath.

It hadn't taken Bennett long.

Hoping Lovie wouldn't cry out, she quietly hurried outside.

Good for him. Good for him. Good for him.

Everyone looked up when she arrived. She smiled nervously. "Should we go back to the store?" she asked tightly. "Lovie is getting fed up. We might think about going home and coming back some other time?" She bounced impatiently on her tiptoes. If Bennett saw them, he'd come out and introduce his friend. Sisley wasn't ready for that. Not yet.

"Oh." Sam's smile slipped. Her eyes went to Lovie. Sisley glanced down too. Lovie was full and content, lying on Sisley's chest like a happy little slug. Not a thing about her said she was fed up.

Kimmie pulled her chin back and raised a questioning eyebrow. Sisley shrugged lightly, letting Kimmie know that yes, she understood it was awkward. Still. Let's go.

"Sure, Sis. Let me go pay. That'll be faster than waiting for the kid in the sneakers," Travis said. In front of him stood an untouched coffee, but no cake. Apparently, even carrot and lemon had run out.

"No..." Sisley closed her eyes for a moment. The register was in Bennett's line of sight. If he broke eye contact with his friend for even a second, he would see Travis waiting for the bill.

She opened her eyes again. "I'm sorry. You just got your coffee. It's okay. It's not... Lovie's fine a little longer." She pulled a chair around, so she sat with her back to the café. "I'm sorry. Never mind."

Kimmie's other eyebrow rose, and Sisley nodded that it was okay. Change of plans. She was just being ridiculous.

She *was* being ridiculous. Bennett wasn't hers; they'd settled that. They were only friends.

"Uh..." Kimmie said and pointed over Sisley's head.

"Sisley?" Bennett's low voice made her close her eyes. "What are you doing in Beach Cove?"

She took a moment before turning around. "Bennett! Hi." Her voice was almost normal.

His eyes were guarded. "Hello...everyone. What's happening?"

"We're visiting," Kimmie said. "What are you doing here? Hi!" She smiled at Bennett and then, at Bennett's friend.

"Oh." Bennett stepped aside so the woman could join him. "This is Sophia. Sophia, these are friends from Bay Harbor. And, uh..."

"Sam Bowers and Martin Sullivan," Sophia filled in. "Hi." She seemed as guarded as Bennett. Maybe Sisley's first impression had been wrong.

"Long time no see, Soph," Sam said. She didn't sound too sorry.

"Are you leaving soon?" Bennett asked, looking at Sisley. "There's a thunderstorm coming. If you want to take the shortcut over the cliff, you should probably get going."

"Hmm." Sam tilted her head. Sisley saw her lock eyes with Sophia. Some communication occurred between them, and then Sam slapped her hands on the table, pushed her chair back, and stood. "It is true. The sky's getting dark, and you don't want to get caught on the cliff when there's lightening. Maybe it's best to get going." She checked her phone. "I better get Martin back, too."

"What?" Martin looked up. "I think we...oh." He, too, met Sophia's eyes. "Yes, maybe we better..." He stood laboriously and held out a hand for little Brooke, who reached up and took it. "Can I have a number?" he asked Sisley. "I would like to get in touch again. I would like to—" He huffed as if catching a sob or a gasp or maybe, something in between. “I sure would like to meet your mother.”

“Yes,” Kimmie said before Sisley could. “We’ll need to talk more.”

He smiled, looking from sister to sister. Sisley held out a hand, and he took it with his free one. “Thank you,” he said. “I’m old, and my memory doesn’t work the way it used to. But I think I will remember the moment you walked into my store.”

CHAPTER 16

Mela ended the call, sat in the armchair in her living room, and looked at her daughters. They were sitting across from her on either side of Sunny on the sofa, dipped in the eerie light of a thunderstorm about to break. Lovie lay swaddled on Sunny's lap, contently sucking on a pacifier. After sleeping in the car, she'd protested against the solitude of her usual early-afternoon nap in the upstairs crib.

"Well?" Kimmie asked and tickled Lovie's tummy.

"Well." Mela shook her head to clear it. "I think we need another DNA test."

"So you believe him?" Sisley looked up.

"I don't see why he should make up a story like that." Mela picked up one of the pink macaroons Amelie had dropped off earlier, frowned at it, then set it back on the plate. Her stomach felt like a pit full of sawdust.

She couldn't believe it had been that simple. Why had they not told her?

"I already ordered the tests," Kimmie said.

"I have to peel the last of the apples before they shrivel," Sunny squinted longingly in the direction of the kitchen and shifted Lovie into Kimmie's lap.

"It'll be okay, Sunny," Mela said automatically. "I can't believe I have a *grandfather*."

"Of course you do," Sunny said and stood. "We just didn't know who it was." She started to walk toward the kitchen. Suddenly, she turned around and clasped her hands. "I'm sorry, Mela. I'm so sorry."

Mela's head was still swirling with everything the candy shop owner had just told her. But the expression on Sunny's face pulled her out of her thoughts. She forced a smile for her aunt, who looked miserable. "What about? You have nothing to be sorry for."

"I should have guessed." Sunny kneaded her fingers into a ball. "I should've realized he wasn't her brother."

Mela felt her smile relax. "Goodness, Sunny, I should've guessed it too. Maybe not back when I was little, but sometime after. Like when I learned Constance never mentioned Finn once. Who wouldn't mention her son?"

Sunny blew out a breath. "There were rumors."

Mela tilted her head. "Rumors?"

"About Julie and Finn." Sunny shrugged. "Small-town rumors."

"That they weren't brother and sister?"

Sunny blinked. "Julie was so upset. Usually, she'd laugh off something that stupid. I was surprised she cared so much about rumors." She frowned, her shock melting into anger. Mela couldn't tell whether Sunny was more annoyed with Julie or herself. "Turns out she lied to me. Her own sister."

"Well, Julie didn't know you were her sister," Mela said reasonably.

Sunny tossed her head. "*Half* sister."

"Goodness. Half sister. Fine. She still didn't know, Sunny. I'm sure it'd been a load off her shoulders had she known she had a sister. She was fighting on several fronts there. Constance, Finn, having a baby by herself..." Mela understood how Sunny felt. But thinking about all Julie had tried to do on her own, at twenty-four, broke her heart. She could feel anger rise and breathed it away.

"Well. If *I'd* known, I'd have given her a piece of my mind. She knew everything about *my* situation. I never would've shared that knowing she was holding out on me." Sunny's mouth puckered.

Mela had never seen her aunt like this. She didn't know what to say.

"I think Julie was scared of Finn's ex. She didn't like conflict. And she sure didn't want to be the one who caused Melanie to lose it and take it out on Finn's little girl." Sisley was looking at her hands, but the frown line running between her eyes was still visible. "Don't be mad at Julie, Sunny. She doesn't deserve it."

"You're right," Mela said softly. Her youngest was so much like Julie. "I know in my heart Mom did the best she could. Either way, it doesn't matter anymore."

Sunny dropped her hand in sudden defeat and sighed. "I miss that woman every day."

"I remember it was overwhelming when you first saw the house," Mela said. "How is it now?"

"Being here helps, actually. I'm closer to her here." Sunny spread her hands as if she could touch Julie's spirit. "But there's no closure."

"No," Mela agreed. "There'll never be closure. But I hope we at least find a clue as to what happened. Somebody must know something."

"Tell us again what happened," Kimmie said.

"I was kept in the dark about a lot of things," Mela said after a while. "But I was told that they took out the boat Finn had built. I gathered from a note in Julie's journal that he wanted to take Amelie and me too. A family trip with my best friend for company, I guess." She scratched her forehead. How strange that sounded. How strange it was to think of it like that. Her dad had wanted to take her too, so she might be part of his proud moment. "But Mom was determined to test the boat first."

There was a moment of silence as they thought of Julie, and of what had happened, and what could have happened.

"Oh thank heavens, Julie," Sunny said, and the words rang with a new conviction. "She made sure you were safe. I'm sure she was so grateful you were safe when she realized what was happening."

"I don't know," Mela replied. "Ever since I read that note, I've wondered whether Finn would've stayed closer to the coast had we girls been in the boat."

"You had no choice." Kimmie's eyes widened. "Don't put that on yourself, Mom. None of it was your fault."

"I guess not," Mela murmured. "A little tweak here or there and their lives might have been spared. It's so easy to play what-if."

"But not very productive," Sunny declared sternly. "I think I need a moment. I'm going to peel apples." She left. A moment later, they heard the kitchen radio play a Greek group-dance song.

"It's a bit much for her," Mela said. "She didn't see that one coming. Me neither."

"I wonder what happened to Melanie," Kimmie said.

"She died quite a few years back," Mela repeated what her new and presumed grandpa had reported. "She couldn't tell the police anything. She didn't know Finn had a boat, or where he was." She straightened her shoulders. "What I would like to know is what happened to her daughter Kitty. My..." She cleared her throat. The words felt strange in her throat. "My half sister, I suppose?"

"Did Martin not know?"

"He said they fell out of touch after Finn's disappearance. Melanie eventually remarried and wasn't interested in staying in touch with Martin. They'd already moved to Vermont. Back then, that was far away. And Martin was grieving."

"Do you know Kitty's last name? I can probably find her on the internet," Kimmie said. "Everyone but Peter is on social media. She'll have a Facebook account, or she's on Twitter or Instagram."

"What about me?" Peter walked into the living room, pulling his sweater over his head. He smelled of honey and beeswax and smoke. "What's going on here? Did someone die? Where's Sunny?"

"She's fine." Mela opened her arms, and he bent to kiss her. "Did you go to the field?"

"I put the swarm in a new hive." He smiled. "They sure don't like a thunderstorm coming their way. I got two stings—hey, what's that look?"

"I found out who my father is," Mela said and launched into the story of the kids going to Beach Cove. Peter sat beside her on the arm of her chair. "I just got off the phone with Martin," Mela concluded.

"Whoa," Peter said and turned to the kids, who were still sitting like chickens on the sofa. "You ladies be careful digging around the past, please."

"Martin is literally a ninety-year-old candy maker," Sisley said and smiled. "I think we're okay."

Peter looked at Mela and inhaled to say something when the front door opened and fell shut again. "Mela? You'll never believe this!" Amelie's voice came from the entrance hall. A boot clattered to the floor, and they listened while she struggled to get the second one off. "I heard a rumor Bennett was seen with a *gorgeous* woman in Beach Cove!" The second boot dropped. "Maybe now that he and Sisley—oh. Oh."

"Hello, Amelie." Peter grinned at his old friend. "Come in."

"Hush, Peter." Mela's eyes went between Sisley and Amelie, who now stood at the door, her eyes on Sisley's fixed smile while embarrassment started to drag down her own.

"It's all right," Sisley said. Her voice was carefully neutral. "Bennett and I are just friends."

Amelie's gaze went to Mela in search of help.

"Today's a day for rumors," Mela said calmly. She didn't like the way Sisley looked. "Sometimes, that's all they are."

"Sometimes, they're true too," Sisley replied coolly. "Like the one about Finn. And we saw her too. She *was* gorgeous."

"What about Finn?" Amelie plopped down on the couch beside Sisley and took her hand. "You know I'd love nothing more than you and Bennett dating, sweetheart. But if you don't want him, then..."

"Yes. Of course," Sisley replied hastily. "Of course." Her cheeks flushed.

Mela cleared her throat. Poor Sisley...if only she could have met Bennett before Lars. The two of them would have been perfect for each other. But her last relationship had changed Sisley. Only she could know what was perfect for her now. "Amelie. It turns out Finn was not my uncle. He was my *dad*. Allegedly."

Amelie's eyes widened. "Wowzah. Tell me everything."

The story was told one more time. In the end, Mela waved an exhausted hand. "Another DNA test will tell. Kimmie's going to take one over to Martin."

"More family," Amelie said. "Small towns, eh? I'm surprised, but I'm not surprised."

"I'm sure Martin's telling the truth," Sisley said. "I saw his face. He's not one to spread rumors."

Sunny stepped into the doorframe, drying her hands. "I can't concentrate," she declared. "Let's all go air out our heads on a beach walk."

"It's raining," Kimmie pointed at the window. "Thunderstorm and all that."

"We have raincoats for everyone," Mela said and stood. "I could use some airing out. Come on—it'll be fun to walk in the rain by the sea."

There was some grumbling and protesting and what-about-if-lightning-starts, but in the end, everyone found a more or less waterproof jacket, and even though there were not enough duck boots to go around, Mela promised to throw all wet sneakers into the dryer afterward.

They set out, walking through the dripping field until they reached the sea. Their heels left deep impressions in the wet sand, and the stormy waves eagerly filled them back in. Grouping and regrouping in pairs and threes, they discussed the news.

"It'll be okay," Mela promised Sisley when they had their moment. "Look." She bent to pick up a piece of green sea glass as big as a piping plover egg.

Sisley made an effort to smile. "How pretty. To think it was a bottle shard once, right?"

"Here." Mela pressed it into her daughter's hand. "With time and patience, even sharp edges turn into something beautiful."

"Are you talking about glass shards or Bennett?" Sisley held out her hand, the palm glistening with rainwater. Zipped inside her wax jacket, Lovie stirred as if she wanted to see.

"I have no idea." Mela closed Sisley's fingers over the gift. "The times where I could teach you anything are well over."

Sisley's eyes softened with humor for the first time since Amelie's grand entrance. She hooked her arm under Mela's and ducked her head against the rain. "Come on, Mom. Let's see whether I can't find some sea glass for you."

They caught up with the next group, Amelie and Peter, who were walking arm in arm. Peter offered his other arm to Mela, and she took it. Four-in-a-row, they made their way across the freezing beach. "What happens next?" Peter called over the rising wind.

"I want to see Martin," Mela called back. "I should go to Beach Cove."

"I'm coming," Amelie yelled, leaning around Peter to see Mela. "Let's go tomorrow, okay? I don't have any appointments."

"I'm coming too," Peter yelled. The sea reared her foamy horses against the wind as if the two had a battle.

"We're all going," Sisley screamed. "But right now...hot chocolate and marshmallows?"

"Sounds good!" Mela laughed, the sounds ripped from her lips as soon as they formed, and they broke apart and turned back, leaving the rest of the group to come to their senses themselves. It was fast walking now that they were sailing with the wind, and soon they let themselves, laughing and chatting and dripping wet, into the kitchen.

Mela handed out towels and warm socks and oversized sweaters, and by the time Kimmie and Sunny returned, blousy and frozen, they had started a crackling fire and had hot tea waiting for them.

"Here's to small-town rumors," Mela said and raised her mug. "They keep life interesting, to say the least." The others followed, and then the front door opened again, and Travis and Pippa appeared dripping wet at the door.

"Kimmie." Travis pushed his hood back. "That's where you are. You didn't answer your phone. I was worried you'd tried to go back to Beach Cove."

Kimmie looked around. "Oh goodness, I don't even know where my phone is! I'm sorry. I think I left it upstairs in the nursery."

Mela looked at Pippa and thought the moisture on her cheeks wasn't only rain. She stood and went to the little girl, taking her from Travis. "Come in, you two." She wiped Pippa's cheeks dry with her sleeve and unzipped her coat. The girl was terrified that something had happened to Kimmie. In her small world, loss was only too likely. "Do you want hot chocolate?"

She nodded.

"Come here, sweetheart." Kimmie opened her arms, and Pippa went to her and climbed on her lap, nestling her head against her, and Kimmie pulled the couch throw over the two of them.

Mela looked at Travis to ask if he wanted tea, but he wasn't paying attention to her. His attention was on his daughter and Kimmie.

"Come on in, Travis," she said quietly and held out a hand for his wet jacket. "There's space for one more on that couch."

CHAPTER 17

The storm raged and roared through the night, and it took three days before the street to Beach Cove became halfway passable. Peter stopped the car on top of the cliff.

"How beautiful." Mela opened her door and got out. "You can see almost the entire cove."

The rain had washed the last summer dust off the land, and beach and sea sparkled like sapphires.

"Most of the land up here is private," Peter replied. "It's a pity. This is the only spot where you can pull over for a view."

"Honestly, I wouldn't sell either if this were mine," Mela replied and hooked her arm under his. "This spot is small but certainly good enough for a view."

"I do wonder whether Bay Harbor would get more visitors if this road was better," Peter answered. "Nobody even knows there's a vista point up here."

"A sign might help," Mela agreed. "Who do you have to petition for street signs?"

"The town, I guess. But I'm not sure out-of-towners can do it."

Mela smiled. "Maybe long-lost grandfathers can. Talking about... Should we go? The others will be there already."

"Yes." Peter leaned over and kissed the top of her head. "I'm starving too."

Not much later they reached the small harbor, where colorful lobster boats and fishing vessels bobbed on the water.

They parked and strolled toward the restaurant where they were to meet the family. "I can see why tourists come here," Mela said. "Bay Harbor could be this cheerful too if there was a bit more money to go around."

"The old chicken and egg." Peter opened the door for her. "We need tourists to turn it into a good tourist destination."

"One piece of that puzzle at least is back in place now that the motel is renovated. All we need is for visitors to find it."

It'd been cooler outside ever since the storm, and the warmth inside felt good. It smelled of roast garlic and seafood, and the buzz of conversation greeted them. All tables seemed filled with families and couples, but a waitress waved them on. "There are the kids." Peter waved, and Mela craned her neck.

In the back, several tables had been pushed together. Around them sat Sisley, Kimmie, Johanna, Morris, Travis, Sunny, Amelie, and Meredith. Little Pippa was in a highchair, and even Lovie was propped up on Johanna's lap.

"There they are indeed." Mela stopped to take in the sight. Sometimes it was still unreal to her how much her chosen family had grown. "Look at them."

"That's our kind of real estate," Peter said. "We don't own a gorgeous cliff, but we have acres of good people in the family."

They made their way to the table and were greeted cheerfully. The waitress arrived with the drinks and warmly recommended the clam chowder. They ordered a big pot with sourdough bread sticks to share, as well as flounder and fried clams and too many lobsters, sharing and swapping the savory dishes. When they were done, Mela and Peter snuck to the register to pay, their departure unnoticed in the general noise.

"You're Martin's granddaughter, aren't you? I'm Sharon." The waitress held out her hand, and Mela shook it.

"I'm Mela. And this is—"

"Peter, right?" Sharon held out her hand for him too.

He took it and smiled. "How do you know?"

"Everyone knows everything in Beach Cove. I'm sure it's not too different in Bay Harbor." Sharon tapped at the register and printed the bill, then took Peter's card. "You're the owner of the Bay Harbor Motel, aren't you?"

"I only just found out about this place," Peter said, sounding incredulous. "How do you know about the motel?"

"Rumors for starters and the internet to follow up." Sharon smiled back at them. "Your daughter gave me a stack of cards. They're almost all gone, and it's not even the season. If you have more, I'm happy to keep handing them out. I don't like having to say no when people ask if there's a place to stay around here."

"I do have cards." Peter scribbled his signature and then pulled a stack from the breast pocket of his suit. "Thank you."

"You bet. Us fishing towns need to stick together." Sharon glanced at her tip. "Thank you. Very generous. But you didn't have to. I'd still hand out the cards."

"We have a big party, and the food was delicious." Mela liked the woman. "I'm glad we came."

Sharon leaned on the counter. "I know you renovated."

Peter nodded. "We did. The place is all dressed up with nowhere to go."

"How is the town doing for restaurants?"

"There were a few, but they're barely surviving," Peter replied. "We only have a couple left now. They're desperate for business too."

"You know what, go talk to the ladies over there." Sharon pointed.

Mela turned to look. Four ladies in their early fifties were putting their heads together to talk among themselves. There were empty plates and full chardonnay glasses in front of them.

"What about them?" Peter was looking too.

"The lady with the silver hair and the curly brunette beside her—they're Maisie and Ellie. They run Beach

Cove's inn. They're overrun with requests for rooms and have to turn most of them away."

"I heard of them," Mela said suddenly. "They once gave a canceled room to Johanna. Who are the other ladies?"

"The pale, tall one is Sam." Sharon smiled fondly. "Try and get on her good side if you can. Maisie will listen to her. Ellie, too, though she doesn't like to admit it."

"Sam was helping Sisley in the candy store," Mela said. "I'd love to meet her."

"The fourth one is Cate. She'll help you no matter what. The three others can be a bit difficult, but they're all of them nice enough. Good luck." Sharon patted the counter and returned to her duties.

Peter eyed the table. "What does she mean by difficult?"

"We'll see," Mela said. "Let's go talk to them. Do you have any more cards on you?"

Peter did, and they made their way to the table. The four women stopped talking and looked up.

"Sorry for interrupting. I wanted to say hi—and thank you. You've helped out my girls when they came here," Mela said.

"You're Sisley and Kimmie's mother," Sam said. "I see the resemblance. Nice to meet you."

"And Johanna belongs to you too. She stayed with us not long ago." Maisie smiled.

Mela nodded. "I'm Mela Beckett. And this is Peter Townson."

"Nice to meet you. Sorry for interrupting your lunch."

"No problem," Cate held out her hand. Mela shook it, and then Peter. "Sam just told us about Finn and Julie. Would you like to sit down for a moment?"

"For a moment, yes. We have the kids back there." Mela pointed toward their table. The four ladies turned to look. Kimmie and Sisley were doubled over laughing, Johanna and Amelie seemed to be arguing over something, and Travis was rocking Lovie while listening to Pippa explaining something while she held up bits and pieces of different foods and then stuffed them in her mouth with relish.

Peter pulled two more chairs to the table. "We're from Bay Harbor," he told Maisie and Ellie. "I own a motel over there."

Ellie put her elbows on the table and her head into her hands. "It used to be run down," she said critically.

"We've just finished renovations." Peter pulled out a card and laid it on the table. On it was a photo of the new motel in all its glory. "I was hoping you could come to visit someday and have a look. If you like it, I'd be grateful for your recommendations to people you have to turn away."

"Ah, we can use that." Maisie picked up the card and studied it. "We'd like to visit. Thank you."

"The road over the cliff is very pretty," Cate said. "Too bad it floods easily."

"That's only at the bottom, though," Sam said. "My friend owns most of the land up there. I'll see whether she can help get the flood zone fixed. She usually gets what she wants. I just don't know whether she wants a lot of traffic up the cliff. Her mother certainly didn't—but she's moved away."

"If you put in a word for us, it could help our town get back on its feet." Mela smiled her thanks.

"Are you here to meet Martin?" Cate asked. "I saw him this morning. He was in his Sunday best, and we were wondering what had gotten into him. Your visit would explain it."

"Yes, we are going to meet." Mela checked her phone for the time. "And we should probably leave. I don't want to be late." Nerves fluttered in her stomach.

"It's all right," Cate replied. "Time moves slower here. People don't get mad if you're a little late."

Mela smiled. "I still have to get used to that. Being on time was so important in my old job, and old habits die slow."

She and Peter thanked the four friends, returned the chairs, and joined their own party.

"What happened?" Amelie leaned over the table, eyes curious. "Who are they?"

Mela told her. "They seem nice. Maybe they'll send some guests our way."

Amelie repeated the information for Meredith, who didn't hear as well anymore, and then Meredith told Johanna, who elbowed Kimmie, who elbowed Sisley, who told Morris. The three girls who met the ladies before stood and waved hello across the restaurant, and Sam, Maisie, Ellie, and Cate waved back.

"Okay. I'm going to go," Mela announced. "Amelie and Peter, will you come with me? You also knew Finn."

"A little bit," Amelie threw in. "We've seen him a couple of times thirty years ago."

"Same." Mela sighed.

"Sure," Peter said. "I'd like to go."

Morris stood too. "I'd like a look at the boats. Anyone coming with me?"

Travis and Pippa also wanted to see the fishing vessels, while the women decided to stroll the quaint streets. Johanna looked torn but then decided against love and boats and in favor of girlfriends and cute stores. Mela covered her smile at Morris's disappointed expression and made everyone agree to meet at the marketplace fountain in two hours.

The streets were empty enough now that the season was over, but the little stores were still tempting. They strolled down Main Street. Mela's nerves started to flutter the closer the time came to meet her grandfather.

"This must be it." Amelie pointed at the marquise. "Striped like a candy cane."

"Yes, that's it." Peter went and opened the door, waiting for them to go through.

"Ooh," Amelie said softly, looking around the store. "It's like the German Schlaraffenland."

"What's that?" Mela's heart was beating in her chest. The store was empty of people other than themselves. Had she gotten the time wrong after all?

"It's a German fable of a land where all you do is eat," Amelie explained, trailing along the shelves and tables of candy. "It's paradise, but you have to eat your way through a mountain of pudding to get there. Not everybody makes it."

"They get stuck in the pudding?" Peter ascertained.

"Yep."

"Does it trap them like flies in amber? What sort of pudding is it?"

"I don't know. It might have been cake."

"But can they get back out the way they came?"

Amelie sighed impatiently. "That's not the *point*."

"Not my idea of paradise," Peter remarked, making up his mind about the fable.

"They came up with the idea of a Schlaraffenland before there was fast food," Amelie hissed under her breath. "When little villages barely had enough to eat to make it through the winter."

"You know, or you think?" Peter whispered back.

Amelie rolled her eyes in exasperation and popped a saltwater taffy sample into her mouth.

A floorboard creaked. Mela wheeled around.

From behind the honey-colored counter, an old man was looking at her with eyes as blue as her own. His voice shook when he spoke. "Mela?"

She nodded. "Hello, Martin," she said, and her voice trembled too. "It's good to finally meet you."

CHAPTER 18

The movie pirate wobbled as if he were drunk, but a sharp glance from his dark-rimmed eyes belied his clumsiness. Pippa giggled and Kimmie smiled, her eyes meeting Travis's over the girl's head. Pippa had snuggled in between them, pulling the blanket she'd dragged from her room over the three of them.

"Do you like the pirate?" Travis asked his daughter.

"Yes! He's funny. Look. He fell into the water." She giggled again.

"I think he's funny too," Kimmie said.

Pippa plopped to the floor, rolling on her belly and pulling the blanket around her like a cocoon.

Travis stood and put another piece of wood on the fire. It crackled and spit and smelled of tree sap and Christmas. "Pine," he explained. "Loud, but it's nice and dry and doesn't smoke."

"Hmm." Kimmie fished another pecan shortcake cookie off the plate on the coffee table. "I have to stop eating these. I'll be so out of shape."

Pippa scooted closer to the TV to hear the actors over the interruptions.

"You're in great shape." Travis returned and sat back in his spot beside Kimmie. "I bet you can outrun me."

Kimmie nibbled on her cookie. Sisley was singing Lovie to sleep upstairs, the soft pitch of her lullaby audible every now and then, and Morris and Johanna were sitting in the dark at the dining room table. They'd come in late from a walk by the sea and missed the first round of dinner, catching up on the roast and mashed potatoes while talking quietly and gazing into each other's eyes.

For all intents and purposes, Kimmie was alone with Travis.

Their eyes met.

"Are you okay?" Travis asked quietly.

She lowered her cookie. "As in?"

"As in...us."

Kimmie's heart slowed. "Us?"

"I mean Pippa and me. Us being here." Travis looked away. "Quite literally taking your space in your house."

"Oh. Yes, of course." For a moment, she'd thought he meant the two of them. Her and him.

His throat moved. "We haven't talked about—any of it."

"We don't have to, Travis." She put the cookie on her napkin on the table. "It's all right. I promise. I'm...over it. The divorce, I mean." She hoped he would look so he could see her smile.

He nodded once, folding his hands between his knees. Then he turned his head, meeting her gaze. "I'm not," he whispered. "I handled things badly. I failed. I failed you. Tina. Even Pippa." He blew out a breath, and his eyebrows drew together. "I'm so sorry."

"What? No." Instinctively, Kimmie held out her hand, and after a confused second, he took it. It was cold and familiar. "Okay." She took a breath to brace herself. "I'm not going to lie, Trav. You did hurt me with the divorce. The way you did it hurt even more."

He nodded. His hand twitched as if he wanted to pull it away. "I know," he murmured.

"But I'm good now. I know what happened, and I know that in your situation, I'd have been overwhelmed too." With each word, Kimmie's throat felt drier.

"I knew I was in the for the long haul," Travis said, glancing at Pippa. "I thought I was moving to England for good and that we'd never see each other again."

"I would've thought the same."

He shrugged uncomfortably. "The thing is—I was wrong. Life is not an Edwardian novel, is it? We don't have to marry just because we have a kid together."

"Well, it's quite nice, though," Kimmie replied. "I mean, if you like each other."

"Maybe we don't have to get divorced either, just because we have a child with someone else."

Kimmie's throat was parched. She tried to clear it but couldn't. "I suppose not," she whispered, sounding as if she'd crossed a desert. "But it is good to know. I mean, for the partner." She inhaled. "I mean, it's nice to know whether your partner has kids."

"It is nice to know if *he* knows." Travis, too, looked like he had trouble swallowing. "*If* he knows."

Kimmie let go of his hand. "He knew," she whispered. "For an entire year, he knew and didn't tell me."

Travis looked down, and then it was he who took her hand. "I was a coward," he said. "I had no idea what to do, and so I..."

Kimmie waited, her heart drumming to a beat she thought she'd lost.

Travis lifted his head. "And so I did the wrong thing, Kimmie. I should have called you. I mean, I tried, but you were in a war zone. Something in me clicked into the wrong place, and all my anger and rage at the situation was suddenly directed at you." He pressed his lips together. "None of it was your fault. It wasn't Tina's either. The anger was all my own, just because I'd been thrown a curveball."

"I guess so." Kimmie unfolded her leg from under her. "I'm sorry, Travis. I think I have to... I should probably go upstairs."

His eyes held hers. "I've learned a lesson, Kimmie. Don't run away when it gets difficult."

Kimmie was poised mid-air for a moment, but then she sank back on the couch. "Okay. Let's do the difficult bit right now. I don't know how long I'll last."

She saw relief softening his lips. "Once I got a grip, all I could think of was you. How I should ask you to come live with me and Tina and Pippa."

"Uh, not sure about that one," Kimmie said. She thought of herself as a modern woman, but not modern enough to live with her husband's ex and their love child.

"It wasn't like that," Travis whispered, lowering his voice so Kimmie could barely hear him. "Tina wasn't in love with me. Never ever for a second. She needed me to take care of Pippa because I was Pippa's father. That was all there was between us. Well—there was friendship too, at the end. I did what I could for her." His throat moved as he swallowed. "She was grateful I stepped up, Kimmie. If you'd been there...you'd know what I mean." He rubbed his face. "There never was anybody for me but you. I don't expect anything. I just wanted you to know. That's all." He turned away as if looking at her was too much.

Kimmie sat frozen. That was all? What did he mean, that was all?

"You have some nerve, Travis," she whispered when she found her voice. "You have some nerve, telling me that."

He sighed. "Is it selfish to say I still love you? Should I keep to myself that I've loved you all along?"

"Yes," she hissed and stood. "Yes! I've—"

Pippa looked up, frowning. "Shh."

Kimmie sat back down, and Pippa looked back at the screen.

"Everything all right?" Morris asked from the dining table.

"Sure." Kimmie waited until Morris turned back to Johanna. "I love you too, Travis," she hissed more quietly. "I've loved you all along too, and I've learned to live with it. You can learn to live with it too!" She karate-chopped a pillow in her anger, and Travis's eyes opened with alarm.

"You sure you're all right over there?" Now Johanna's eyebrows were raised.

"Yes!" Kimmie said loudly. Suddenly, she was furious. She wanted to punch Travis's arm for doing this to her. "Yes, I'm fine." She glared back at him. "I'm going upstairs. Don't stop me again."

He nodded. "That's how I felt. I was angry like that—just more. Much more." He stood to make space for her so she could leave. "I'm sorry."

Kimmie stormed past before the tears rising in her throat would spill. Not because she was sad; she didn't cry when she was sad. She cried when she was spitting mad.

Taking the stairs two at a time, she ran upstairs, reaching the corridor before recalling that she didn't have a room up here, in her own house, because she was staying at Mom's. The wave of wrath crashed over her head. "There's no place for me!" she yelled.

Downstairs, she heard shuffling, and then someone ran up the stairs. "Morris! Get away from me!"

"It's me, Kimmie. Travis." He appeared.

Speechless, Kimmie shook her head; she didn't want Travis. She never wanted him again. Tears ran over her cheeks, wet and vulnerable, and she wiped them away with angry jerks.

"Come." Travis caught her in his arms, and suddenly Kimmie was too busy sobbing to fight him off. "Shh," Travis said. "It's all right, Kim. We got this. Calm down."

He led her into her bedroom.

His bedroom.

"I don't even have a space in my own home," Kimmie repeated, hearing how petty it sounded and not caring.

"Pippa and I will leave tonight," Travis promised. "There's plenty of room at the motel."

"No." She fell on the bed and curled up in a ball, pulling the cover over herself like a wounded animal hiding from the poacher.

"Yes. It's too much." Travis sat beside her, his weight pressing on the mattress.

"No," Kimmie repeated. "You're *staying*. You're *staying* because I say so." She threw the cover off and sat up. She wanted to force him to, this once, do exactly as she said. "You're *my* husband, and you're staying here because *I* say so."

His lips twitched as she glared at him. Then he reached out and, with the back of his hand, wiped her tears from her cheek. "Am I?" he asked.

"Are you what?"

"Am I your husband?"

Kimmie pressed her lips together to keep from falling apart entirely. Her anger and its energy were gone as suddenly as it had overcome her. It felt as if she'd penetrated the storm and was now in the very eye, where it was calm and quiet and most dangerous.

"*Am* I your husband?" He stopped drying her tears and simply sat there, looking at her.

"Yes," she whispered. "I'm sorry, Travis."

"I'm not sorry." He leaned in and pressed his lips to hers.

The center was crossed, the eye behind her. The storm broke once more over Kimmie with a force she hadn't foreseen, a power she hadn't reckoned with and couldn't withstand.

Her husband's hands and his mouth, his strong body and whispered words, were the only shield she had to protect herself from the elements threatening to crush her. She had no choice but to surrender completely, to let him take over so she might survive.

CHAPTER 19

The early-morning breeze nipped like a naughty puppy. Amelie pulled her lined trench coat closer around her and shivered as she eyed the eight-feet metal fence topped with barbed wire.

"Waiting for a plane?" The young woman who'd been pottering with a tiny two-seater plane walked up to her. She was holding a jacket in her hands as if she couldn't feel the October cold.

"My friend said to pick him up. I've never been to a private airport. Should I come in? Should I wait here?"

"You can come in if you like. Where's your friend coming from?"

Amelie shrugged helplessly. "Sydney."

The woman laughed. "I bet he didn't fly his plane all the way around the world. If he did, he wouldn't be landing here. He probably chartered something small in Boston or Portland."

"Maybe that's him?" Amelie pointed at a plane humming closer.

The woman squinted at the sky. "Could be. Nobody else is out here this morning."

They watched as the plane dropped and landed, making Amelie's coat flutter.

"You still want to come in?" the woman called over the noise of the dying engine.

"I'm all right. Thank you." Amelie couldn't take her eyes off the airplane. "Charlie! Hey! Charlie!"

He appeared at the door and jumped down to the ground, laughing and waving at her. Another man took his seat in the cockpit, and the airplane rolled to a parking spot while Charlie strode to the gate.

"Amelie." He pulled her to him.

She hugged him back, her heart beating harder. "Are you here to stay?"

"I'm here to stay." He let go again, and she stepped back, heart drumming.

How did one give a second chance? Where should they start?

"Let's go home," she said. "Is that all you have?" She pointed at the backpack slung over his shoulder.

"It's all I need for now," he replied. "I thought I'd wait with the rest until..."

She held on to her purse. "Until when? Until you know for sure you want to stay?" she asked. The wind pulled a strand of hair over her face.

Charlie tucked it back behind her ear. "Until *you* know. I already do."

"Oh." Impulsively, she stood on tiptoes and pressed a kiss on his lips.

He broke the kiss, and she dropped back on her heels. Neither one of them said a word as they held each other's gaze.

"What about now?" Amelie swallowed, nerves fluttering in her stomach. She couldn't read his expression. "Do you still know?"

Suddenly he was grinning like the high school boy she'd known all those years back. "Careful," he warned and put an arm around her shoulders. "I'm not as sweet and innocent as I once was, Amelie." Without further ado, he pulled her into him and pressed a long kiss into her hair.

"I guess I should be careful then. I don't recall you ever being sweet and innocent."

"Not with you." His grin faded. "Not with you, buttercup."

Buttercup.

"Build Me Up Buttercup" had been the last song at their prom night, when they'd held each other, swaying in circles too slow for the rhythm, their eyes making forever promises to each other. Heat rose in her cheeks, and she shook her head, laughing at herself.

"My car is parked over there," she said and took his hand. "Are you staying with Peter?"

He didn't answer until they reached her car. "Yes," he said. "For now. But I didn't come here to live with my brother."

Amelie nodded. She knew it'd be better to ask later, when things between them crystallized. But after losing three decades, she was impatient to speed things along. "So, um...what happens if..."

The corner of his mouth tugged upward. "If I mess up my second chance with you?" He looked up into the sky as if the answer might be written in the sparkling blue fall morning. "Oh well," he said finally. "I'll just have to buy my own beach house and go for a third chance, I suppose."

"Three chances?" Now it was her who was grinning.

"I'll take my chances as long as you let me." He winked at her, making Amelie laugh.

"We'll see," she warned and unlocked the doors. "I'm not so sweet and innocent anymore either. Maybe you don't like the new me. Maybe we'll find out that we'd rather just be friends."

They got into the car. "Rather than lovers?" he asked, and then he chuckled at the look she gave him. "Does that sound weird?"

"Yes!" Amelie put her face into her hands. "*Feels* weird."

"Do you think of me as Charlie or a stranger?"

"It changes every other second."

"So the kiss was..."

"A second when I knew exactly who you are."

He chuckled. "Let's see which side wins. You can always change your mind, Amelie. If it helps relieve the pressure, I wasn't joking about getting my own house. I've already reached out to my real estate agent, and she's looking around."

"Thank you." She looked up, and he smiled back.

"Drop me off at the motel?"

Her stomach sunk with disappointment. "There's plenty of guestrooms at the house. I was being serious about giving you a second chance too."

"Never invite a stranger into your house. We've got time." He reached over, his hand bringing the scent of diesel engine and adventure, and touched Amelie's cheek, trailing slowly along her jaw and pushing back the hair so he could see her better. Whether it was the burning trace he left on her skin or the scent, it didn't calm the flutter of Amelie's heart.

She swallowed and started the car. "Can I have dinner with my stranger tonight?"

"In fact, you have to. Wherever you like to go."

"I was going to cook." She glanced at him.

He raised an eyebrow. "What happened to five dates and a nightcap? My carefully laid plan was not to scare you by going too fast."

"Ugh, no," she said, surprising herself. "We've waited so long already, Charlie. Let's do dinner at the house. Mind you, we'll have a chaperone. Our son is going to be there."

"I'd love to see him. Wow. A family dinner."

"My mother might come too," Amelie said. "I'm pretty sure she would like to ask us a question or two. And when I say us, I mean you."

"Ah. Well, I suppose we might as well get it over with."

"Can you play canasta?"

"Canasta?"

"Yes."

"I'm a fiend at canasta," he said. "All those lonely nights in the outback with a bunch of cowboys around the fire and nothing to do. We're experts at any card game you can name."

"Uno?" She smiled at him.

"Especially Uno."

She flipped the blinker. "I have a feeling that you and Mom should be able to establish a working relationship."

"I'm determined to charm her."

They had reached Bay Harbor. The maples lining the narrow street flamed red and golden, and finally, Amelie was starting to warm up. "Good idea," she confirmed. "Mom has changed a lot, by the way. Her life was no straight road either, and it's made her much more tolerant."

"I've always liked Meredith. Even when she didn't like me."

"You did?"

"We had one obsession in common."

Amelie couldn't help but laugh. "Stop it, for crying out loud."

What little strangeness there had been between them was melting in the heat from the vents. Amelie asked about the ranch and how Charlie felt about leaving Australia, where he'd built his life, and Charlie wanted to know about her job and Bennett.

Amelie dropped Charlie off at the motel, watching from the car as Mela and Peter came out of the motel and embraced the long-lost brother. Peter and Charles waved and went inside while Mela came to the car. Amelie lowered the window.

"Everything okay?" Mela squinted at her.

"Everything's great," Amelie confirmed. "Though, to be honest, I thought he'd want to stay with me. But I guess I have to wait my turn. He wants to take it slow."

Mela smiled. "And you?"

"Honestly..." She sighed. "Why wait? Wait for what?"

"Speed it up then. I doubt he'll mind once he tosses the pedestal he's put you on."

Before Mela had returned to Bay Harbor, Amelie missed having a girlfriend. "You're that friend who'd help me bury a body, aren't you?" she asked fondly.

The corners of Mela's mouth dropped like those of a connoisseur appraising a wine. "Depends. Who is it?"

"Nobody yet. But keep checking in."

Mela tapped her hand on the open window frame twice, as if she were rapping her knuckles on a table. "I'll keep checking on *you*."

"Okay." Amelie smiled. "Thank you. Bye."

"Bye. Make something yummy for that dinner tonight, and tell me how it goes."

Amelie started the car. "I'll lock myself into the bathroom and text you." She waggled her eyebrows.

Mela grinned. "Make sure you do. If I don't get an update every two minutes, I'm calling the cops."

Amelie waved and drove off. Love and secret letters and second chances were all very good—but there was nothing quite like laughing with a best friend.

When she pulled into her driveway, she remembered that Bennett was home. He'd put in a lot of extra hours over the jeweler's case, and the chief had ordered him to catch up on sleep while a colleague took a turn at catching the guy. He wasn't happy because the colleague in question was more related to the mayor of Sandville than he was experienced, but Amelie knew her son still needed those hours of shuteye.

"Bennett?" Amelie called when she entered the house.

No answer.

It wasn't a peaceful silence. It wasn't the cozy, comfortable feeling the house usually had.

Amelie tiptoed upstairs and listened at her son's door. There was not a snore nor a creak coming from his room. She knocked, gave it a moment, and then opened the door to peek inside.

The bed was made, the room empty.

She went to the window and looked out into the yard. It, too, was empty.

For a moment she stood lost in thought, trying to remember if he'd said he'd go anywhere.

But no.

She pulled out her phone and texted him. *Where are you?* Then she sat on the bed and waited.

Bennett usually texted back right away. He knew she only texted if she needed an answer.

After ten minutes had gone by without a reply, Amelie rose again.

Maybe the rumors were true. Maybe he did have a girlfriend in Beach Cove. The small town was known for its spotty reception.

Frowning at her phone, she left Bennett's room, leaving the door wide open.

CHAPTER 20

"Your paintings are getting good, Sis." Morris shook his head as if he couldn't believe his little sister had painted something he liked. "I mean it." His breath condensed in the cool morning air.

"Thank you kindly, dear brother," Sisley said politely. She pushed Morris's cup of black coffee away so it couldn't spill on her newest work and dipped her badger-hair brush into the burned yellow she'd mixed on her palette.

Fall had flicked its magic wand over the field, and the unmowed grass swayed in a hundred different shades of gold in the late-morning sun, dotted white and yellow and purple where fleabane and wild asters flowered in all the exuberance of late bloomers.

"I *told* you," Johanna said proudly, rocking Lovie in her arms and peeking over Sisley's other shoulder. "I told you she's marvelous."

"Can I have the painting when you're done?" Morris asked.

Sisley smiled up at her brother. He'd never asked her for anything as far as she could remember. "Sure," she said. "But where are you going to put it? It doesn't exactly go with Peter's motel decor."

"I'm thinking about buying a house, actually." Morris glanced at Johanna.

"Oh?" Sisley lowered her palette. "For real? You're settling down?"

"I can't hog Peter's dining hall forever. He's had some calls about booking rooms, and I'd like to get out asap. And yes. I suppose it's time to settle down."

"I didn't know that, Morris," Johanna said quietly.

He ran a hand through his hair. "*I* didn't know that. It only came to me this morning when I heard Peter on the phone tell someone about the amenities."

"I think it's a great idea," Sisley said quickly. "Have you looked at the housing market?"

"One of the two houses between Mom and Kimmie would be nice."

"Oh! That's what *I*..." Johanna took a breath. "*Oh*."

Sisley looked up in surprise, seeing their eyes had locked. "Really? You want to be that close to family?"

"That way, I have at least one neighbor who will put up with my music," Morris explained. "Plus, I'd like to look out at the sea while I play, and there are not too many houses with a view."

"That makes sense," Sisley said loyally, though she felt a sting of jealousy. She had secretly hoped that one day, one of those two houses would be *hers*. But she had no money and no education for a job that would make enough money to pay a mortgage. She had hoped to get a cashier's job, but the couple who ran the market didn't need help.

"Kimmie had a good real estate agent," Johanna said. "I think his name was Ian? She's got his contact if you want it."

"I talked with Ian this morning." Morris cleared his throat. "Kimmie had shared the contact when she bought."

Sisley returned to her painting. "And? I always wondered whether those houses are for sale or not."

"One of them sold recently," Morris said. "The other isn't listed for sale, but Ian said he knows the owner and will ask if they'll consider selling. I'm waiting for them to get back to him."

"Which one?" Sisley turned back to her painting so her brother wouldn't see her face. If Morris bought the last available house, she couldn't even dream of buying it herself anymore. She couldn't stay with Kimmie forever, either. Judging from the way her sister looked at Travis, Kimmie would soon need her house for herself.

"The green one next to Mom's. If the lilac weren't so thick, you could see it from the patio here." He craned his neck.

"You could cut a path through the bushes from one house to the other," Johanna said, also eyeing the lilac. "That way, if you have kids, they can go visit Grandma."

"That's a great idea, Jo."

Sisley let her palette sink. It wasn't that she didn't want Morris and Jo to have that. But she craved giving it to Lovie too. She wanted Lovie to have the luxury of a path through the lilac by the sea too.

But her siblings had worked hard and long for that luxury. Sisley had only been busy drinking Lars's Kool-Aid. She'd made her bed, and now she had to do her best to like it.

"It *is* a great idea," she said as firmly as she could and lifted the palette back up. "I hope it works out, Morris."

"What's going on with Bennett?" Johanna suddenly asked. "I haven't seen him in a while."

"Me neither," Morris said. "Sisley? Do you know?"

She misplaced a white dot. Her brother was starting to irritate her with his constant interruptions. "Why would I know where he is?"

"Oh, that's right," Morris said with the emphasis of a lightbulb moment. "He's got a woman in Beach Cove."

Sisley stood. "I think I'm done," she said and started to pack up her things. "I'll finish it later."

"Oh. Can't you do it now? I was looking forward to taking it with me."

Sisley sighed. "You have first dibs if you still want it when it's done, Morris."

Johanna kissed Lovie's head. "You know, Sisley, you should start selling these. I'd pay good money to get one. You should be a professional artist."

"Yeah right." Sisley shook the water from a clean paintbrush. "I don't think being an artist is going to pay for Lovie's diapers."

"No?" Morris sounded surprised. "Why shouldn't it? I've always done all right."

"You're semi-famous," Sisley said reasonably. "I'm a college dropout."

"First, I *am* famous. Nothing semi about it, other than that my family has no clue," Morris corrected her. "Second, people aren't hanging your college degree on their walls but your paintings."

Sisley smiled at him. "Thanks for saying that, Morris. It makes me feel a little better."

"I didn't say it to make you feel better. I think you should go for it, Sis. Find a gallery that will put your paintings up. See if something sells."

"I wish." Sisley wiped her fingers on her rag. "No gallery will take on a no-name like me."

"If you don't have the guts to ask, I will."

"Sure." Sisley needed to nurse Lovie, who was whining and making faces. She took her from Johanna. "Knock yourself out, Morris. If you get me a gallery, I'll get a portfolio together."

"Where's the closest gallery?" Morris asked Johanna.

Jo rubbed her biceps. The baby was heavier than she looked. "Sandville, probably. Bay Port will have several."

Morris shook his head impatiently. "Why doesn't Bay Harbor have a gallery or a venue for concerts? No wonder we don't have enough visitors."

"I would *love* a bookstore," Johanna said dreamily. "I'm staring at the screen all day. I want to read a real book on real paper in my spare time."

"Hey." Sisley turned to her brother. "Your piano is already hogging the motel's dining hall. Just put a few chairs around it and call it a concert. The guests could even stay at the motel afterward."

"I like it," Morris said slowly. "Tell me more."

She hoisted Lovie higher. "That's all I have. But you can figure it out. I'm serious."

"I'm serious too," he replied. "I can't sit on my laurels forever either, especially if I want a...house. I'll talk to Peter. I don't want to play in a motel forever, but I want to stay in this town. That's what you have to do too, Sis, if you want to stay and live off your art. Start small. Start somewhere. As long as you make it real."

Sisley looked at her brother. His words lit a flame of hope inside her. Unlikely as it was to work out, if she could make a living as an artist in Bay Harbor... "Morris, I'm in," she said.

She couldn't give Lovie the luxury of lilac walks to Grandma's house. But maybe she could show her daughter how to follow a dream.

"Good." He narrowed his eyes as if he was looking for something in her face.

"Morris, I'm serious. I want this. I didn't know it until you said it, but now I do. It's like I finally understand."

She expected a grin or a quick comment, but instead, her brother suddenly pulled her into his arms and kissed the top of her head. "I know the feeling," he murmured. "I know it well. Be smart. Use it, but don't let it burn you up." He let go.

"Let's open a venue to show art and have music. Nothing fancy. Coffee, popovers, and paintings during the day, and jazz in the evenings. What do you say?"

"Yes *please*," Johanna whispered. "That would be great. We could have readings too. I bet lots of authors would love to come and spend a few days writing by the sea."

Morris squared his shoulders. "Let's do it, Sis." He held out a hand. "Let's go into business together."

Johanna clapped her hands. "It's going to be great! There's nothing to do in the evenings but look at the sunset or watch TV, and there are only so many times you can go out to eat. People would be grateful for a reason to come together!"

Sisley swallowed the excitement rising in her throat. "You too, Jo. You could organize readings."

"Yes! And you know what? One of my clients is a mystery writer who lives in Maine. I'll ask if she'll get us started!"

"Hold your horses, you two." Morris laughed. "First, we need a place."

Sisley shifted Lovie. "We'll ask Peter and Charlie. I'm sure they'll let us use the dining hall until we can rent another space. In return, we'll drum up business for the motel."

Mentioning Charlie made Sisley think of Bennett again.

"What? What's that face?" Johanna had noticed.

Sisley shrugged. "Bennett is mad at me," she said. Suddenly, it was easy to admit. "He decided we can't be friends if we..."

"If you can't be more?" Johanna guessed.

Sisley nodded. "He needs to do what he needs to do, but I miss having him."

"As a friend?" Morris asked. "You can't lead him on forever."

"I'm not leading him on," Sisley said sternly. "This isn't a Victorian ballroom. I like him very much, but I'm just not ready for another relationship."

"Morris, hush. That's very reasonable. She just had a bad breakup and a baby," Johanna said. "Of course she needs to take her time."

"But you like him," Morris said. "I know it. I've seen you with him. He's nuts for Lovie too. You'll never find a better dad for her. What am I missing?"

"I don't...trust him?" Sisley shook her head. She'd never explained herself.

"Don't trust *Bennett*? Goodness, Sis, he's the only person in Bay Harbor you *can* trust, and I include Mom."

Johanna laughed at the exaggeration, and even Sisley had to smile. "I know," she said. "I don't know how to explain it."

"You don't trust yourself. That's the problem," Morris said. "I was like that before I went into rehab."

"I hardly think—"

"And I was like that after Mom passed away," Johanna said. "It was hard to even look at anyone. I was so afraid I'd get hurt for losing them."

Morris held out a hand. To Sisley's surprise, Johanna took it, and Morris brought her fingers to his lips and kissed them. “I’m getting better.” Johanna blushed like a bride.

“Are you two dating?” Sisley tilted her head. “I mean, we all knew you two would eventually—am *I* missing something here?”

She was even more astonished when Morris laughed and pulled Jo to him. “We might be,” he said, and Johanna smiled weakly. “We might’ve been dating since the party in the orchard.”

“Sorry, Sis,” Johanna said. “I wanted to tell you, but it never seemed to be the right time.”

“Plus, trust issues.” Morris squeezed Jo, and she giggled. “We all have them. Get over yourself—and Lars. Don’t let him dictate any longer what you do or don’t do. Don’t give him that power.”

“I just thought...” Sisley hesitated. “I thought I needed to stand on my own two feet for a while. Take care of Lovie without relying on anyone else.”

Morris spread his hands. “Why would you think that? Who are Mom and I and Kimmie? Chopped liver?”

“No, of course not. But I can’t live off others forever.”

“That doesn’t mean you have to ignore what we offer,” Morris said. “From artist to artist, Sis—it’s better to have a heart and break it again and again than to not have a heart at all.”

“I don’t know what that means,” Sisley said. “And I have a baby. I have to function. Which I won’t, if my heart is constantly broken.”

"Bennett wouldn't constantly break your heart, though," Johanna pointed out. "I think you're snow-balling."

"Admit it, Sis." Morris pointed an accusing finger at her. "Constructing reasons not to be in love with him only makes you unhappy. Him, too, I might add."

"When have you become so insightful?" Sisley frowned.

"Rehab," Morris said resignedly. "They made us think this through. It was terrible."

"You're really the worst..." But already, he'd made Sisley laugh again.

"Do you like Bennett? Enough to go on a date?" Johanna, tucked safely under Morris's arm, smiled at her.

"Yes," Sisley said without thinking. "If I didn't have to be so careful, I'd say yes."

"You don't have to be careful," Johanna promised. "That's all Lars talking. Take your voice back, Sisley. Date like Lars never happened."

Something shifted in Sisley's heart.

If Lars had never happened, she'd be in Bennett's arms now.

She dropped her head. "He's seeing someone in Beach Cove. Her name is Sophia. His interest in me didn't last that long."

"Or, maybe, get out of your head and ask him if he's still in love with you," Morris said. "You can't expect him to moon around. And he's too good to let go without even asking."

"Talking about Beach Cove," Johanna said suddenly. "Kimmie's tests arrived. We should go over to Beach Cove and see Martin. He wants our help so he doesn't mess it up."

"He's ninety, and *he's* trying his best," Morris said. "That's how you do it, Sisley. You're scared to mess up, so you ask for help and do it anyway."

Sisley sighed. "I'll go to Beach Cove if you go," she said. "Maybe that's where Bennett is."

"Yes, maybe that's where Bennett is," Morris said distractedly, pulling out his phone with his free hand and scrolling with his thumb. "He's not answered my text asking if he wants to go fishing. It's his day off, and we said we'd go before it gets too cold."

"I also sent him a text and haven't heard back." Johanna frowned. "My author client has a question about police procedure. I thought he'd be happy to help out."

"Sisley? Have you heard from him?" Morris looked at her.

"No," she said, feeling her heart sink as if an anchor was dragging it down. "I'll call him right now."

She did. The call went straight to voice mail. "His phone is off." Without missing a beat, she looked up his station and called to check if he was working after all.

"No," a detached female voice replied. "Detective Cobb isn't in today, and we're not expecting him for a couple of days."

"Okay. Thank you." Sisley ended the call.

"Nothing?" Johanna looked worried.

Sisley shook her head. She inhaled, willing herself to stay calm. Of course there was a good explanation. Maybe he was meeting Sophia. Maybe, for once, he had turned off his phone and wasn't making himself available to everyone at all times. He certainly deserved it. But...

"Let's go to Beach Cove for lunch," she heard herself say. "Maybe he's hanging out in the café again. I just want to know he's all right. If we see him, we wave and move on. We don't even have to talk to him."

"Don't worry," Morris said. "He's all right. If anyone can handle themselves, it's Bennett."

"I just have a funny feeling." Sisley pressed a hand to her stomach.

"Don't want that." Morris stretched, and then he took Lovie from Sisley. "I have nothing planned for the day. Jo? Fancy a stroll through a quaint seaside town?"

"Sure." Johanna put an arm around Sisley. "It'll be okay."

Sisley nodded but didn't answer. It didn't feel okay. "Let's go right now," she said. "Let's pick up Kimmie and Travis too. It'll be good to have them." They were investigative reporters, after all.

"If they got up yet." Johanna grinned.

"What?" Sisley tilted her head. "Already?"

"Last night. I swear." Johanna nodded significantly. She pulled out her phone and sent a quick text, then read the reply. "Kelly and Laurie, Kimmie's real estate agent and her sister, stopped by to say hi and see the kids. Kimmie says to nurse the baby and be ready to surrender her. They want a turn pushing the stroller and taking Pippa to the playground."

Johanna and Morris went ahead inside to change Lovie while Sisley quickly washed out the last brushes and, in her mind, went over the supply of bottled milk. Suddenly, she looked up. She'd heard something.

There was nobody. She was alone.

Only the wind moved through the dry grass, swift like a person running. *Hurry*, the ripe stalks seemed to whisper. *Hurry, child.*

CHAPTER 21

Mela exhaled and tugged the sleeves of her oversized Irish cable-knit sweater over her hands. It was cold on the patio; enough for her breath to mist the morning air. Fall had settled in, and it wasn't going to get warm again. The winds of the last few days had taken down masses of leaves which were now dancing in the streets and sidewalks.

Her chat with Martin when they'd visited Beach Cove had been short. A busload of tourists had found their way into the store minutes after Mela, Peter, and Amelie introduced themselves and shook hands. The energetic group had been noisy, loudly calling for each other's attention and asking Martin an endless stream of questions.

Martin had promised to return the visit, insisting the drive would be no trouble.

Mela checked the time again.

"Come inside," Sunny called from the living room. "Let's close the patio door."

"Not yet." Mela pushed the sleeves back up. "I can't decide if I'm too cold or too hot."

"You're too *nervous*." The logs crackled and thumped as she stirred the fire. "I made a fresh teapot and my special apple pie with candied walnut crumb and whipped vanilla cream."

"Perfect. Thank you."

"*I'm* cold. Come inside."

Mela turned to do as her aunt said when the doorbell rang. "He's here!"

She hurried to the front door and tugged it open. "Martin!"

The old man smiled. He was leaning on a wooden walking stick that looked like a short staff. "My dear Mela. It's so good to see you."

"You too, Martin."

A middle-aged woman with curly brown hair and blueberry-blue eyes, dressed in jeans and a navy knit sweater with the image of a red lobster stitched on it, peeked around Martin. She gave a short wave. "Hi. I hope you don't mind I came."

"Hi," Mela smiled at her. The woman would be Martin's ride. Mela immediately liked the open face, the wide smile, and the laugh wrinkles brightening the woman's eyes. "Come in, you two."

She helped Martin out of his fisherman's pea coat, busying herself with hanging coats and purses and pointing out where their wet shoes should go.

Moments later, everyone sat on the couches in the living room.

"This is my aunt, Sunny." Mela introduced them. "Sunny, this is Martin, and this is—" She smiled an apology.

"Oh. I'm sorry." The woman moistened her lips. "I'm Kitty."

"Kitty!" Mela stared at her, thunderstruck. "*That* Kitty? My sister?"

Martin cleared his throat. "I asked the detective who handles Finn's case to find Kitty for me and give her my contact info. The detective did." His eyes twinkled. "Kitty was on Facebook all along. The problem was, I wasn't. She'd been looking for me too, turns out."

"I'm sorry. I thought you knew I was coming. Martin, you should've told her! It's a bit of a shock."

"I did! Didn't I?" Martin scratched his head. "Oh, maybe I didn't. I apologize, Mela."

Mela put a hand to her heart. "So you are my *sister*?" she repeated. Her voice shook. Everything felt unreal.

"If you really turn out to be my dad's daughter, we should be half sisters." Kitty smiled.

Mela nodded. "Sunny, did Kimmie's tests come already?"

"I'll have to ask her." Sunny cleared her throat. "I know how hard it is to wait." For the next ten minutes, she and Mela told them how they'd found out they were niece and aunt. Kitty and Martin relaxed as they ate their cake and listened to the story.

"It all started with your return," Kitty said to Mela. "You're bringing together a family that was scattered by sadness and secrets."

Mela burned to know more about Kitty, but she didn't want to be too forward. Maybe for Kitty, their shared parent was a painful topic. "It can't have been easy for you," she said carefully. "Not having your dad when you grew up, I mean."

Undaunted, Kitty met her eyes. "My mother wasn't well. She had mental health issues, and unfortunately, she was unwilling to take medications. She didn't like the way they made her feel, poor woman." Kitty's smile didn't falter. Mela understood that she was setting the tone for how her mother was to be talked about.

"I understand," Mela replied. "Medications back then probably had lots of side effects."

"Oh yes. It wasn't easy." Kitty leaned back. "But I still had my grandmother. I could go to her when Mom wasn't able to care for me." A wisp of a frown touched her face before it left again. She seemed like someone who remembered the difficulties of the past but had come to terms with them. "When Mom remarried, I moved back to Maine with my grandmother. I still live just a skip and a jump away in Seal Harbor."

Mela had always wondered how it would have been, had she been able to stay with Constance. Or, even better, if Sunny's attempt to claim her had been successful. "I'm glad you were okay."

"I certainly was," Kitty declared. "At least I still had some family. And now I have more." She took Martin's hand and smiled at Mela.

Martin blinked. "Look at me," he said quietly. "Sitting here with two granddaughters. And I thought I was a lonely old man."

"I do hope we're right," Mela said. "I don't quite dare to let myself believe I have a grandfather and a half sister before we see the tests."

"There's more evidence for it than we had, Mela." Sunny leaned into her comfy chair, the picture of contentment. "We only had a photo and a feeling. Martin knows what happened. He knows who you are. You don't need the test."

"I'm—" Mela struggled for words until she laughed. "I'm so *happy*. Especially that you came so I could meet you." She turned to Kitty. "It hasn't sunk in yet that we're sisters. It feels unreal."

"I know." Kitty grinned. "I have a little sister. It's so strange, isn't it?"

Sunny and Martin jumped in with stories about Julie and Finn, and the old times came alive again. They saw a young, single mother in love with a man who was married, rejected, and loved again before building a boat that turned out to be a grave.

"They were just babies," Sunny concluded. "I see that now. We were all just a bunch of babies trying to do the best we could."

"Both you and your mom had secret half sisters," Kitty pointed out. "Think it runs in your family?"

Mela chuckled. "My daughters know exactly how many sisters they have. By the way, what is it you do, Kitty? I would like to know more about you."

"And I about you." Kitty poured herself another cup of tea. Mela didn't know what her sister did for a living, but she already saw that Kitty was a grounded, straightforward person. The kind of older sister Mela had missed all her life. "I'm a hatmaker."

"A what?" Mela leaned forward.

"I make hats. People custom-order them from all over the world, and I make them."

"I love that." Mela had never met a hatmaker. Now it turned out she had one for a sister. "It sounds like a big business."

"Not so very big, but enough to make a living." Kitty smiled.

"Do you have a store?"

"It's mostly online. My dream is to open an atelier, but I live in Seal Harbor. I can't afford the rent."

"Oh, I see." Seal Harbor had developed into a small but eclectic and extremely expensive resort town ever since a famous talk show host had bought a house there. Her many guests liked what they saw, and one by one, properties were purchased and old houses razed to make space for mansions.

Kitty bit the inside corner of her mouth. "I'm slowly but surely priced out of the town. I have my grandmother's bungalow, but it's falling apart no matter how much money I put into it. I can't afford to rent an apartment these days, let alone an atelier." For the first time, Kitty's eyes veiled with worry.

"Move here," Mela said suddenly. "Move to this lovely little town and join us. We need more people, and we need small businesses. I need a sister. And houses are still comparatively cheap."

Kitty looked up. "Actually, it has crossed my mind before. I lease a stand at the farmers market here. It's a great market, but I only come once a month anymore because there are not enough people ordering hats for weekly trips."

"I love that market. I'd hoped to sell my honey there and even got all the licenses I need. But getting a stand is a problem. The lady running the show didn't give me much hope of success. She said I'm on a waitlist several feet long."

Kitty smiled. "It's harder to get a foot in the door now than ten years back. But Mela, the guy who shares the rent and uses the stand when I don't has mentioned returning his part to me. I could get you in, if you'd like."

"Yes! Let Kitty help you," Martin threw in with his creaky voice. "That's what sisters do."

"I agree," Sunny said and went to get more cookies.

"Really?" Mela turned back to Kitty. "I don't want to cut in the line."

Kitty shrugged. "It's my stand, and I can do what I like with it. That's how it works in this market. Of course they don't tell that to newcomers." She leaned forward. "Let's give it a try this coming weekend. We'll set you up for a test run and see how it goes. It'll be fun."

"Oh. Kitty. I would love that. It's been on my bucket list since I was a kid and my mother came home with a hive in the back of her car, talking about how we would sell honey and live happily ever after."

"Aww. Well, that settles it. Do you have honey ready to sell?"

Mel nodded. "Ever since my first conversation with the market lady, I've been mulling over jars and ribbons and labels. I didn't think I'd get a stand, but I still made plenty just in case."

"She made enough for all of Bay Harbor," Sunny piped up. "I told her it was too much."

"Atta girl," Martin said proudly. "We've always sold sweets in this family. It's my Finn coming through."

Mela winked at him but didn't point out that honeybees had been Julie's dream. "Great!" she said, squelching the squeak of excitement bubbling in her throat. "Thank you, Kitty. Let me know what I owe you. I know the rent is not cheap."

Kitty tilted her head. She looked out of the window, and then she looked back at Mela.

"How about a trade?" she asked. "Maybe I could come stay with you the night before the market. I usually have to drive up in the middle of the night to be ready when the market opens." She grinned her charming grin again. "I'm not much of an early riser. And..." She cleared her throat, her blueberry eyes twinkling in the light of the fire. "I've always wanted a little sister. I'd like to spend some time together."

Mela swallowed. "I've always wanted a sister too, Kitty. You're more than welcome to stay with me. I'd love for you to meet my daughters."

The twinkle in Kitty's eyes spilled over. She hastily wiped her cheek. "Sorry. Yes." Her voice was firm and clear. "I'd *love* to meet your girls."

"Can you two stay for lunch?" Sunny asked, sounding a little choked up herself. "I'm making halibut and new potatoes."

"We used to have a great fishmonger in Beach Cove. Her halibut was outstanding," Martin said, a wistful look on his face. "But she retired. Now the fish store is a bakery, the fishmonger runs an inn, and good halibut is rare."

"I think we might know her," Sunny said. "This halibut is fresh from the boat. We only have a couple of commercial fishermen left in Bay Harbor, but they do know their business. I'll ask them to make sure to catch more halibut so you can have some too."

Martin's face brightened. "It's all the sweets around me all day," he explained. "I need something savory for my meals."

"Do you cook much?" Sunny asked. The tone in her voice told Mela her aunt was already turning over plans on how to get meals over to Beach Cove.

They chatted until it was time to make lunch, and Peter and Charlie joined them just before Amelie arrived. Sunny quickly pan-seared the fish in lemon butter and reheated the roasted crushed potatoes she'd already prepared while Amelie showed Mela and Kitty how to make a new creamy dill sauce she'd created. Through the open kitchen door came the voices of the brothers as they told Martin about a large group of guests who had booked rooms at the motel, and he in turn told them some outrageous stories from the candy store.

Mela sampled the dill sauce. "Have you heard from Bennett?" she asked.

"No." Amelie frowned. "The kids think he might be in Beach Cove, meeting with the woman everyone's shipping him with. Sophie? Sophia."

"Shipping him?" Kitty looked up. "What does that mean?"

Amelie brushed her hair back. Even though they were not related, Mela thought Amelie looked more like Kitty's sister than her. "It means they root for you to be together. My teenage clients explained it to me."

"Who does? I don't get it." Mela dried her hands on a kitchen towel.

"Like Mr. Darcy and Lizzy in Pride and Prejudice," Amelie elaborated. "We, the readers, ship them. We want them to end up together."

"Aha. By the way, do you know where the *kids* are? Other than Bennett, I mean."

Amelie stirred the dill sauce one more time. "They drove over to Beach Cove this morning. I only know because Sisley texted to ask if I wanted her to check for yellow napkins over there. They were sold out in Bay Harbor before I'd made up my mind to buy them, and there's another branch of the store in Beach Cove."

"And did you?"

Amelie shook her head. "No, but it was kind of her to ask." She lowered her wooden spoon. "I wonder what the kids are up to," she said.

"Are they up to something?" Mela looked up at the same time as Kitty and Amelie.

"Do you have a bottle of wine?" Amelie asked after a moment.

"Yes, I do," Mela said, stepping on the feeling of unease that was rearing its head.

"Beach Cove is a sweet place," Kitty said calmly. "I'm sure they're fine."

A throat cleared behind them, and the women turned to look. The men were standing at the door, and Martin looked as if he wanted to say something.

"Yes?" Mela smiled at him.

"I wouldn't say Beach Cove is a *sweet* place," Martin said thoughtfully. "Not exactly *sweet*."

CHAPTER 22

Sisley jumped out of the car and scanned Beach Cove harbor as if Bennett was hiding on one of the lobster boats bobbing in the cove. Travis had insisted on driving, and Kimmie, shiny-eyed with pride, had promised he'd get them to Beach Cove faster than anyone else. She'd been right. Only a half hour had passed from the moment they'd picked the two up at Kimmie's house. Laurel and Kelly, who'd stopped by for a coffee, had taken Pippa, Lovie, and an ample supply of diapers, milk, and snacks to the playground.

Johanna and Morris folded themselves out of the car and stretched. "Bit of a squeeze," Morris muttered. Johanna elbowed him gently in the ribs. "Not that you minded."

"Not that I minded." He grinned and snatched her into his arms.

"Okay. What do we do first?" Sisley interrupted them. Between Morris and Johanna cuddling the entire way and Kimmie and Travis glowing with happiness, she had to make sure everyone stayed on track. "Let's spread out. Bennett could be anywhere."

"I thought we were going to the café to grab lunch," Kimmie said, coming to stand by her. "If he's not sitting there in full view, Sis, we probably shouldn't try and track him down. That's stalking."

"It's not...stalking. Is it? Is it stalking? I just want to make sure he's safe. I have a funny feeling."

"Maybe you should have told him about your funny feeling before," Morris said with brotherly callousness.

"Let's just go," Sisley murmured and started walking toward the marketplace.

"Wait for us!" Kimmie and Johanna caught up, hooking their arms under Sisley's.

A few minutes and a steep climb up Marina Alley later, Sisley spotted the marketplace fountain and the café behind it.

"There it is," she said, relieved. She needed to get to the café. Now. *Now*.

"Slow down!" Johanna was in top shape, but now she huffed. "Kimmie, what's gotten into her?"

"Maybe she wants a piece of the good tortes before they run out?" But even Kimmie wasn't laughing anymore. "Calm down, Sis."

"I am calm," Sisley said, trying to breathe normally. She slipped her arms free and passed the fountain without sparing it a look. The sun was shining, but the temperature had dropped here too, and only a few of the café's bistro tables had customers sitting at them.

She turned around. Kimmie and Jo had stopped at the fountain to dip their hands and wait for their men.

Sisley opened the door and stepped inside, quickly scanning over the heads.

No Bennett.

She exhaled, dizzy with the sudden warmth. She had so hoped she'd see him look up with a frown and ask what the heck she was doing in Beach Cove.

"Sisley?"

Sisley turned. "Sam!"

"Are you okay? You look pale."

Sisley cleared her throat. "I'm fine. Just...warm." Her eyes were glued to the woman standing beside Sam by the door. It was Sophia, the woman who'd been with Bennett.

"Sisley, you remember Sophia, don't you? She's one of my best friends."

"Hello again." Sophia narrowed her eyes at Sisley but held out a hand.

Mechanically, Sisley shook. Sophia's handshake was firm and decided. The woman knew what she wanted.

"Hello."

"We were just leaving," Sam explained and glanced at Sophia. "What brings you here, Sisley? You don't look like it's the good cake."

Sisley took a deep breath.

What did it matter whether Bennett was seeing Sophia? At least Sisley would know he was okay. She couldn't stand that feeling in the pit of her stomach any longer.

"I'm looking for Bennett," she said. "Have you seen him?"

Sam shook her head at the same time, but Sophia looked up. "Bennett Cobb? Why?"

Sisley turned to her. "He's a friend. Do you know where he is?"

"Is he okay?"

Sisley swallowed. Sophia's immediate concern did nothing to soften her own—and the fact that Sophia thought of his wellbeing first showed that she cared for him. Maybe as much as Sisley did...

Sam cleared her throat. "Sisley, Sophia's also a detective," she said. "Beach Cove is her beat." She turned to Sophia. "Is that what you call it? Beat?"

"No," said Sophia.

Sisley stared at her. "You're a detective?"

"I work a case with Bennett," Sophia said and tilted her head as if a penny had dropped. "That's all."

It was as if the weight of the sea lifted off Sisley's shoulders. Again she felt dizzy, but now it was as if she were a scuba diver ascending from the depths to once again see the light of day. "Oh," she said. "I see."

"Are you okay?" Sophia grabbed her arm as if she expected Sisley to topple over in a faint. "What's going on?"

"Yes," Sisley managed a smile, feeling pathetic for having been jealous. "I'm okay. I'm worried about Bennett because it's his day off and nobody can reach him."

"He just took a couple of days off." Sophia turned her back to the other customers as if she had secret information and was worried about lip reading. "The case he's working on is in my court, so to speak. He was going to catch up on sleep."

"Only he isn't," said Sisley, matching Sophia's whisper. "His mom doesn't even know if he slept at home."

"Does he have a girlfriend?" Sophia pulled open the door and waved Sam and Sisley out.

"We all kind of thought you were," Sisley admitted sheepishly.

Sophia grimaced. "I could be his *mother*, child."

"But you're beautiful," Sisley pointed out. "Nobody cares about age these days."

"I care," Sophia said. "I got through that phase of my life and don't intend to go back. Not even by proxy. Fifty is the new good times. You have sorted out most of your baggage and have halfway decent insurance."

Sam chuckled. "Sophia is one of the best. She'll help you find Bennett."

"No, I don't think so." Sophia lifted a hand in refusal.

"Yes, come on. You told me Bennett was all right. That qualifies as friendship. Be nice and help the girl find him. Look how worried she is." Sam nodded at Sisley.

Sisley held her breath. It was as if something had wrapped itself around her, making her be as still as she could. She suddenly wanted Sophia to help, too. As a cop, one of the best, she would know what to do.

Sophia frowned. "Why? Do you have a feeling?" she asked Sam.

The quiet around Sisley loosened, and she was able to speak again. "*I* have a feeling. I feel like something bad happened."

Sophia ignored her, but Sam threw Sisley a short, sharp glance before returning it to Sophia. "Yes," she said. "I feel like you shouldn't be a jerk, Sophia. Help Sisley find Bennett. Off duty. As a friend. He'd look for you if I asked."

"Ugh." Sophia checked the ugly Casio watch on her arm. "Fine. Let's call him on his work phone. If he sees it's me, he'll answer. Just telling you right now, that's the end of it. I'm not going to ask where he is or what he's up to. I'll pretend it was a butt dial and hang up right after apologizing profusely."

"Thank you." Some of the urgency had left Sisley. "That's totally fine. I don't need to know where he is as long as he's okay. Please call him."

Sophia dialed and pressed the phone to her ear.

Sisley spotted the rest of her crew steer toward them. "Is he here?" Kimmie asked, joining their group.

"No." Sisley shook her head. "Sam is helping me find him," she whispered to her sister. "And Sophia is a detective working with him."

"Ahaaa. See? He only loves you."

"What are you two whispering about? Should we have a seat?" Morris looked over Kimmie's shoulder. "Eat some cake to maybe calm down quite a lot?"

"He's not answering." Sophia lowered her phone.

"What does that mean?" Sisley returned her attention to the two Beach Covians. "Did he switch off the phone?"

"That's not a phone he'd switch off, even on a day off." Sophia shook her head. "But Beach Cove has terrible service," she said. "Half the time, phones don't work here."

Sam nodded. "What's next? Radio or something?"

"That only works if he's working and has his radio with him," Sophia said. "Which I don't expect is the case."

Sisley inhaled. "I called his station. They said he was off duty."

Sophia nodded. "Let's not make this official quite yet."

Travis joined them, wrapping his arms around Kimmie. "I was thinking about going for a beach walk before eating," he said. "Want to join us?"

"Yes," Kimmie said. "I need to walk more and eat less cake."

"A beach walk?" Sisley looked at him. How could they think of beach walks when Bennett was missing?

Sophia ignored the interruption, and Kimmie and Travis left the circle. "Do you know of any other places he might be?"

Sisley tried to think. "He's never said anything about any places in Beach Cove. Maybe if I hadn't..." She pressed her lips together.

"What?" Sam asked. "Tell Sophia. Details matter."

"Details matter," Sophia confirmed.

"He asked me...and I said no." Sisley couldn't get herself to repeat her stupid decision to the older women. "If I'd said yes, I'm sure I'd know where he is right now."

"Kimmie wants to see the beach Finn liked," Travis reported back. "I think we'll leave now. Call us when you want us, Sisley."

Sam lifted her head. "Finn?"

Kimmie rejoined them too. "Last time we were here, Martin told us Finn had a favorite spot. Smuggler's Beach."

"Save yourself the trouble," Sam said. "That beach has been closed for a long time."

"Bennett and I drove past that beach recently," Sophia mentioned. "He even mentioned how the old staircase was rotted and unsafe."

"We just found out that Finn was our grandfather," Kimmie explained, unfazed. "We'll only drive by too. We don't have to go on the beach."

Sisley knew her sister well enough to know that she, like her bestie Johanna standing shiny-eyed behind her, had zero respect for no-trespassing signs. They would absolutely go on that beach. She needed to make sure that... "Sophia, maybe Bennett is on that beach too," her mouth said. "Maybe he, too, wanted to check it out. Let's all go there."

Kimmie frowned and shook her head at her, but Sisley shrugged. "It's a dangerous beach, Kimmie," she said firmly. "I don't want you lot to go missing too."

"I could've done it," Kimmie complained. "I really wanted to see it."

Sophia grinned. "I'd better show them the beach before they go on their own," she told Sam. "Chaperoning tourists is my job description. Are you coming?"

"Don't mind if I do," Sam said. "Only don't tell Brooke. She'll kill me for not taking her."

Sophia shook her head. "That kid likes water too much," she muttered. "Keep a close eye on her."

"What else am I doing?" Sam sighed.

Without waiting, the two women started walking.

"I guess we're going." Sisley threw an apologetic glance at her sister and Johanna. "You two can't be mad at me for not trusting you. You live for adrenaline kicks."

Kimmie's face suddenly changed, and her hand went to her stomach. Travis glanced at her, and Sisley thought she detected guilt in his look.

"Are you okay?" Sisley asked.

The hand dropped again. "Yep," Kimmie said. "Come on, Johanna. Let's go, even though it is a cop-guided tour. At least we get to stretch our legs before we're back in the car again."

"I do want to see the view," Morris announced, and Travis nodded, though his eyes followed Kimmie.

Sisley started walking after Sam and Sophia. She couldn't understand why the others weren't more concerned for Bennett. Would Johanna look more worried if Morris were missing? Would Kimmie walk faster if it was Travis who couldn't be reached?

"That's my truck." Sam pointed. "We'll be faster driving."

"I suppose we should walk back down to the marina to get our car then," Kimmie said resignedly.

"You can all go in the truck bed," Sam said. "Right, Sophia?"

"No, not in Maine." Sophia opened the passenger door and climbed in. "It's forbidden. I forbid it." She slammed the door shut, eyes fixed on the road ahead.

Sam went to the back and lowered the tailgate. Kimmie and Johanna jumped up without a second thought. Travis followed, sitting beside Kimmie. "Are you sure a truck bed is a good idea?" he whispered.

She turned to him. "What?"

Sisley saw him glance down. "Just...because."

Kimmie's eyes widened. "No. It's fine. I'm fine."

"I know. I know."

Morris cleared his throat, drawing Sisley's attention back to him. "I can't risk hurting my fingers. I'm sorry, Jo, I'll catch up and bring the car. Is the beach on a map?"

Sam slapped the tailgate back in place. "Just follow the coast north. Sisley, you're so skinny, you'll fit in the front with us. Come on."

CHAPTER 23

Sisley climbed into the cab, settling between Sam and Sophia. It should've been awkward, squished between two women she didn't know well, but it wasn't.

For the first time since finding out Bennett was gone, she felt safe.

Sophia glanced at her. "It'll be all right," she said, matter-of-factly. "Bennett is young, but he can take care of himself."

"I know. It's just a funny feeling I have," Sisley admitted. "I've never worried about him before. I swear I'm not a stalker."

Sam flicked the blinker. "I know all about funny feelings. In the pit of your stomach?"

"In the pit of my stomach," Sisley confirmed.

"Did you try eating something?" Sophia asked.

Sam laughed as if the remark was an inside joke.

"I did eat something. It didn't help." Sisley thought it safer to answer.

"Of course it didn't. Leave her be, Sophia," Sam said firmly. "The woman needs to search; we search."

"We search," Sophia repeated mildly. The truck thumped over a bump in the street, and she crossed her arms. "You better not have a bunch of stowaways in the back," she said. "They might fall out."

"I would never." Sam checked the traffic and turned toward the sea. "Who do you take me for?"

Sophia sighed, but Sisley smiled. She wanted friends like that too when she was in her fifties. Half a lifetime spent together, knowing each other so well... She turned and looked out the narrow window showing the truck bed.

Travis's arm was around Kimmie, who was laughing. Johanna was laughing too, catching Sisley's eye and waving.

Sisley smiled.

"Stop twitching," Sophia said comfortably. "Or I'll have to turn and look."

Sisley turned back obediently. "Sorry."

She had Johanna. And she had Kimmie; if they would settle in Bay Harbor, that was. Then they would grow old together and have what Sophia and Sam and the other Beach Cove women had. Every story had a beginning.

"Here we are." Sam pulled the truck to the side of a sandy lane. She jumped out, and Sisley crawled out from her spot in the middle. She heard the tailgate lower and the truck sway as people jumped to the ground. By the time Sophia had stretched and yawned and opened her door, the tailgate had been closed again, and everyone was waiting for her.

"Look at you, being here and everything," Sophia said and squinted into the sun. Then she turned toward the sea. Sam had parked on a bluff, and the sea spread below them. "And look at *that*. Sam, when's high tide?"

Sam checked her phone for the time. "Coming in now," she announced. "Another hour and it'll draw back."

"Right. Well, even if we wanted to go on the beach, we can't do it," Sophia announced.

Sisley stared at her. "Please? Just a quick look around? We've come all the way out here."

"No," Sam said and shaded her eyes. "Not when the tide is this high already. It's too dangerous. Have a look from up here." She pointed to the edge of the bluff.

Sisley went closer.

Protected by the natural gate that broke the force of the Atlantic, the water in the cove was fairly placid. But the tide still rose and fell in its eternal dance, and what looked like it could have been a narrow beach below the bluff now was a whirlpool without a sliver of sand. Driven by the relentless force of the moon, the waves pounded the rock rising from the drowned beach.

"Still another *hour* to the top of the tide?" Sisley asked. She couldn't imagine being trapped in the whirlpool below.

"Yes. That's the problem with this beach," Sam said.

"Swimmers used to get smashed into the rock," Sophia explained unhelpfully. "And of course the caves fill with water; it comes in pretty darn fast too. More than a few tourists thought it'd be fun to go caving and next thing they knew they were gasping a last breath, hoping it was enough to get them out."

"Goodness," said Johanna, sounding interested.

Sophia threw her a sharp glance. "Luckily, the old staircase was washed away."

The base of the staircase leading down to the beach had long since been claimed by the ocean. There was no way up or down.

"Then Bennett's not down there." Sisley frowned. She didn't want to imagine Bennett trapped on that beach. "Where are the caves?"

Sam came to look too. "We can't see the caves from up here. Uh. Uh. Sophia?"

"What?"

Sam pointed.

Sisley's heart made a jump when she saw what Sam had spotted. Midway, just above the missing part, the wooden staircase had cracked apart. The jutting splinters were bright, a soft yellow instead of the usual green-tinged brown of pressure-treated wood exposed to the elements.

The staircase might be old. But the break was fresh.

"Someone went down," Sophia said. "Even though the chain on top is in place." She pressed her lips together.

Sisley's heart bumped like something in the night. "We need to check the caves. Sam, how are the caves now? Are they still safe?"

Sam shook her head. "They're almost underwater, I think. If not completely."

"Someone went down there." Kimmie pointed to a clump of delicate beach grass that had been uprooted. "I see slip-sliding tracks going down but nothing coming back up."

Sophia made a sound somewhere between groaning and swearing. "We need to call Maisie. Right now. Come on." She waved everyone back to the truck.

"What's going on?" Sisley asked nervously. There was no more joking around or pretending Sophia cared about passengers in the truck bed. They were barely onboard when Sam pulled back onto the lane, tires whizzing in the sand as she made a U-turn to get back to Beach Cove.

Sophia was dialing on Sam's phone.

"Sam?" Maisie's voice came on speakerphone. "What's up?"

"Are you home?" Sam called over the noise of the truck. "We need to get into your basement."

Sisley held her breath. The basement of the inn? What did that have to do with finding Bennett?

"I'm not home," Maisie said. "Neither is Ellie. Where's the key I gave you?"

"I wish I knew, but I don't."

"Are you alone?"

"I'm with Sophia and Martin's family from Bay Harbor."

There was a short pause that curled Sisley's toes with impatience.

"Vince will let you in. He's at Carriage House; I'll ask him to drive over. It won't take a moment."

"Thanks, Maisie. I'll call back."

A minute later, Sam turned a sharp corner, and screeches of protest came from the truck bed. Sisley twisted around, but everyone was still there.

"Here we are." Sam pulled into a semicircular driveway in front of a magnificent brick mansion with a carmine door. A pretty sign swinging in the breeze said it was the Beach Cove Inn.

"But what are we doing here?" Sisley asked desperately, jumping out after Sophia. "Why the basement? The water—"

"An old captain built this house," Sophia interrupted her as they hastened to the door. "The basement is the entry to a network of tunnels he used to move smuggled goods. One of them connects to the caves on the beach. If someone did go into the caves, hopefully they were smart enough to go on and find the tunnel instead of trying to dive back out. If they didn't..." She took the short distance in a couple of strides and took a breath as she knocked on the red wood. "Then that's not good."

"Wow," Johanna said. "Always go ahead and see if there's a tunnel. That's what I've been saying all along."

The door opened, and a tall, slightly stooping man with white hair appeared. His eyelids dropped as if he were hiding behind them. "Maisie told me," he said and nodded at Sophia. "Go ahead."

"Whoa," Kimmie whispered behind Sisley as they marched through a grand entrance hall and a corridor that gave them peeks at other magnificent rooms. "It's gorgeous."

Sisley nodded. She didn't have time to spare a thought to the inn.

"No wonder it's always booked out, right?" Johanna murmured back. "The guest rooms are just as pretty."

"Here." Vince tapped a number into a lock that hung from a door. It snapped open, and he removed it, swinging the door open. "You have your phones?"

"Yes." Sisley's hand shook as she tapped on the flashlight app. A long, winding staircase led down into a cavernous basement.

"No worries." Vince winked at her. "It's fairly civilized down there. It didn't used to, but we cleaned it up."

Sam went first, and everyone followed.

"I have to write an article about this," Kimmie murmured. "What do you think, Travis?"

"Good article," Travis agreed.

"Maisie won't let you," Sophia replied from the back of the line. "It's a favor to Martin we're down here. She generally doesn't want people to know about this. Stick to Sam, please. It's easy to get lost."

Sam seemed to know where she was going. They hurried through a couple of bigger rooms into a row of smaller ones that turned into a tunnel. Like in a nightmare, more tunnels opened left and right.

"Who'd have thought," Kimmie whispered behind Sisley. "It's like a dream, isn't it?"

"Not a good one." Sisley was starting to sweat in the close air.

Finally, Sam turned into another tunnel. The air got better, and Sisley could smell a twinge of salt and the faint scent of kelp which meant they were close to the ocean.

Sam stopped, barring everyone from moving forward with her outstretched arm, and held up her phone. "Who're you?" she called out loudly, and then over her shoulder, "Does Bennett have red hair? I see red hair."

"Excuse me," Sophia hissed, and Sisley felt herself get shoved into the wall. The skin of her bare shoulder scraped against rock, but she barely felt it.

"Sam, behind me," Sophia ordered. Sisley watched in disbelief as Sophia lifted her shirt and pulled out a gun. "Get them out. Right now."

"Sophia...careful." But already, Sam started to back up, forcing Sisley and everyone to hastily backtrack their steps.

"What is going on?" Travis stepped to the side, letting the women pass.

"I don't know," Sam said. "But when Sophia says jump, we jump."

They hurried back and huddled into the main tunnel.

"I'm *definitely* writing an article about this," Kimmie whispered. Sisley turned her light on her sister and saw her eyes shine almost as much as they did when she looked at Travis.

"It's okay!" Sophia's faint voice suddenly reached them. "Sam? Send the guy back here."

"That's you," Sam looked at Travis. "You okay?"

"Sure." Travis glanced at Kimmie. "Wait here." He dove back into the smaller tunnel.

Sisley whisked after them before Sam could grab her arm. Was Bennett injured?

"Me too," Kimmie's dark mumble came behind her. "Wait here? I don't think so."

"Sophia said the guy only. Don't get in her way, ladies."

Sisley's light fell on Sophia and Travis, kneeling over a shape on the floor. For a moment, her heart sank, and her knees were rubber. But then she caught a glint of red hair.

Not a trace of red in Bennett's hair.

She took a steadying breath, willing her heart to calm down.

"What do you see?" Kimmie asked. "What are they doing?"

"Lucky for you, I'm putting zip ties on a criminal's hands," Sophia replied dryly. "You were supposed to wait in the tunnel." She stood and nodded at Travis. "One, two, three, lift."

She and Travis hauled the red-haired man onto his feet. His head drooped. "I gotta get him out of here," Sophia said. "The tide beat him up good." She started hauling her prisoner toward the group, and they headed back once more to let them pass.

Sam threw her hands up when she saw what was happening. "Maisie is *not* going to be happy," she said. "She'll—"

"Sam," Sisley interrupted her. She rubbed her arms; the cold damp was giving her gooseflesh as much as the thought that Bennett might be lying down another tunnel. "We need to look for Bennett."

"If this guy's here, Bennett might be too," Sophia said over her shoulder. "The young detectives are all hot-heads. Go have a look for him, Sam, but be sure you find your way out again. Hey. None of that." She readjusted her grip on her prisoner's arm and disappeared around a corner.

"Come on," Sam murmured. "There's one other tunnel leading out of the caves. I think."

"You think?" Sisley hurried after her. "Don't you know?"

"Go left here," Sam said. "Kimmie, go right. Only go down to the end of the tunnel and then get back here. Do not go off to the sides, hear me? We'll have to find you instead of Bennett."

"Johanna and Kimmie, you two go together," Sisley ordered. "Watch each other. I can't deal with losing you right now, and I don't trust you won't go exploring." A sharp note of panic marked her words.

"It's fine, Sis. We'll go together; I'll watch Kimmie doesn't get lost. Just make sure to backtrack yourself." Johanna briefly put a hand on her shoulder.

They split up. Sisley took a deep breath and dove into her tunnel.

She could hear the distant thumping of waves breaking on rocks. Her flash reflected off the uneven walls. After what felt like an eternity, she stopped and held up her light. A bump that was taller and bigger than the others seemed out of place, blocking the way. Then she saw it rise into the shape of a man.

She would have been scared if she didn't know that shape so well. Sisley held her phone higher. "Bennett. Are you okay?"

He didn't reply, but already Sisley knew it was him. She stumbled toward him, her light on his incredulous face.

"Bennett!" She threw herself into his arms, and he caught her.

"Sisley?" He pressed her to him. But it wasn't the embrace of a lover; it was hard, too hard; he was crushing the air out of her lungs, making her gasp as he almost lifted her off her feet. "Get that light out of my eyes. I thought you were someone else!" he growled. "How in the world did you get down here?"

"I was looking for you," she gasped, wriggling against his hold. "We searched for you!"

"Are you crazy?" He swiveled and lowered her to her feet, putting her behind him as if she were a chess figure.

"Long story." Sisley caught her breath, ready to launch into it. Bennett was not glad to be rescued; she could see that.

He pressed a hand to her mouth. "Quiet. We're not alone. Who else did you bring? Only whisper."

She dragged his hand off her mouth and glowered at him. "Kimmie, Jo, Travis," she counted in her normal voice, ignoring his demand. "Sam. And Sophia."

"I said be quiet." Then Bennett's shoulders suddenly relaxed and dropped. "*Sophia* is here?"

"She found a red-haired man," Sisley reported. "The tide banged him up a bit. She tied his hands with zip ties. Travis is helping her drag him out."

A sound she'd never heard before escaped Bennett's throat, and he swayed sideways into the rock, then slid down until he sat with his back to it on the floor.

"Bennett? Are you okay?" Sisley squatted beside him.

"I said get that light out of my eyes." He reached for her, pulling her to him.

"Hey!" she protested, but she'd already lost balance. He held her, her head coming to rest on his chest.

"Do you realize how dangerous it was for you to come down here?"

"No," she mumbled as best she could. "Why—" she squirmed into a more comfortable position. "Why are you down here?"

"I had to get out of Bay Harbor," Bennett replied. "I thought I'd grab lunch somewhere, maybe read a good book at the café. But when I pulled into the parking lot, I saw him driving past me."

"The guy Sophia marched off? Who is he?"

"Someone I was supposed to get off the streets quick."

Sisley had read what happened to the jeweler. "Going after him alone, when nobody knew where you were, was...*unprofessional*," she spat, suddenly livid he would do something that stupid. "Why didn't you call Sophia right away?"

He only held her closer. "No reception," he replied. "What was I supposed to do? He'd been hiding, and I wasn't going to risk losing him again; he's too dangerous. I followed him to the beach. We got into a...uh. Yeah. He ran into the caves, and I thought I had trapped him. I had no idea there were tunnels here."

Sisley twisted so she could see his face in the light of her phone. She'd hugged Bennett plenty of times before. But never long enough to study his face. Stubble covered his chin, and barely dried blood crusted his lip. "It wasn't the tide that smashed him up, was it?" She touched the corner of his mouth next to the split lip. It felt dry and rough with salt and blood. But it also felt warm and full of life.

Bennett caught her hand and kissed her fingertips as if it didn't hurt him. "No," he said roughly. "The tide didn't help at all." He shook his hair back, spraying droplets.

"You're *drenched*." The shirt she pressed against was warm—and dripping wet.

"You didn't notice?" He chuckled. "Sorry. I'm sorry. Now you're soaked too."

"I don't mind." Sisley nestled closer. "You feel good, Bennett," she whispered.

"Yeah? Even though I'm wet and I yelled at you?" His hand stroked her hair.

"Don't yell at me." Her eyes closed as she lost herself in his arms.

"No." He kissed the top of her head. "Only when you follow a murderer into an underground maze. Only to keep you safe."

She opened her eyes. "We need to tell the others you're all right, Bennett." Good as it felt, they didn't have time to cuddle. "Sam knows the way back."

He didn't move. "What are you going to do when we get out?"

"Drive back to Bay Harbor, I suppose." She rocked back on her heels, and he let her go. "And you?"

"I need to find Sophia." He shifted his weight and winced. "And I probably should clean up. I'll stay in Beach Cove and take care of the paperwork."

Sisley moistened her lip. She didn't want to leave Bennett in Beach Cove. "Can I do it?"

"Can you do what?" He winced as he got up, as if the red-headed guy had gotten a few good hooks in as well.

Sisley rose too. "Can I clean you up?" She smiled.

He laughed without humor, touching his ribs. "Trust me, you don't want to—"

"I do," Sisley interrupted him. The light of her phone on the floor weakened. "I do want to, Bennett."

Slowly, he dropped his arm. "You do?"

She nodded and reached for his hand. "Yes."

His throat moved, and his fingers closed around hers. Sisley's phone died, and for a long, dark moment they were alone.

"Kiss me, Bennett," Sisley whispered when she couldn't stand it any longer.

She heard him close the bare distance between them, felt his breath brush her neck. “I want to *see* you,” he murmured. She thought he’d grab his phone, but instead the stubble of his cheek scratched hers, and then he was kissing the sensitive skin just below her ear. A shiver ran down her spine, and a sound of longing she’d never heard before escaped her throat. Her head tilted back, and her eyes closed against the darkness as she pressed into him.

“Kiss me on the lips.”

“No,” Bennett murmured as his lips moved along her jaw. “I’m not kissing you on the lips until I can see your eyes.”

Sisley half laughed, half sighed. “You’re...already kissing...my neck.”

“Nobody’s perfect.” He pressed a kiss on her chin, grazing her bottom lip.

“I’m not.” She thought the words more than she said them, but somehow, he heard her.

“Sounds like we belong together.” He stopped what he was doing with a sound of longing that would echo in her mind for years. Sisley felt him step back, the tiny distance between them making her cold.

She took a deep breath. “We do, Bennett.”

For a moment, he didn’t reply. “For how long, Sisley? Until we get out of here?”

Tears rose to her eyes as her heart spilled over. “I love you. I love you forever, Bennett.”

His lips met hers, hard and unexpected.

"Sisley?" Kimmie's voice came echoing down the tunnel. "Hey! Are you still down there?"

They broke apart. "Yes!" Sisley called back. "Coming!"

"Hmm." Bennett ran his thumb over her flushed and tender lips. "Maybe we should stay."

She kissed his scraped fingers. "Let's not. We don't have to hide."

"Hey—Sisley? Everything okay? Where are you?" A light flickered closer.

Sisley cleared her throat. "I have him! Bennett's here! He's all right. We'll meet you in the main tunnel!"

"Ah! Aha. Well, if you don't mind getting on with it, we're kind of over waiting." Kimmie's laugh echoed against the rock, footsteps scuffed, and then it was quiet again.

"I'm not going to hide." Bennett took her hand. "Is that offer to clean me up still good?"

"Yes," she murmured. "I'll run you a nice, hot bath. How does that sound?"

His response was more gasp than word.

"Let's go to your place... Kimmie's house is too full." She expected him to start walking with her, but he stopped her.

"I don't live with my mother anymore," he said. "I moved out."

"What? Are you—is that why you said you'd stay in Beach Cove? Did you move here?"

"I'll *never* move to Beach Cove," he announced with conviction. "This town has way too many secrets for my taste."

It made her smile. "Then where do you live now?"

"I bought a house in Bay Harbor. I want empty beaches and weekends with friends and my family a short walk away."

"A house?" Everybody but her seemed to buy houses in Bay Harbor now. But if Bennett had a house of his own... "That's great! I had no idea!"

"I bought it for you." Bennett suddenly started walking, as if he was eager to get out.

She followed. "Bennett?"

"I'm serious. Well, I bought it for us."

"You bought the house for us?"

"You were supposed to say yes, that day in the attic," he replied. "You were supposed to move in with me. I guess I got ahead of myself."

They walked in silence until they could see the light of the main tunnel.

Sisley wrapped her arms around his waist to stop him. He was bigger than Lars, and more solid.

"What?" He turned to her.

Sisley took a deep breath. "Will you marry me, Bennett Cobb?"

"No!"

"No?"

He groaned. "I ask *you*, Sisley. Don't do this to me."

She laughed and rose on her tiptoes, pressing a kiss on his mouth. "Ask me then," she whispered and dropped back down.

He reached into the pocket of his jeans. A peculiar expression flew across his face, and he stuffed back whatever was in his hand.

"What was that?"

He only shook his head and reached into his other pocket, pulling out something small. Even in the faint light, Sisley could see blue velvet, crushed and wet.

Her eyes widened. A jewelry box.

Bennett stepped so close to her she had to tilt back her head to see his eyes. "Marry me," he said. "Marry me, Sisley."

"I should probably tell you that I have a baby." Sisley smiled. "What about her?"

"She is—" Bennett's deep voice dropped another notch. "I couldn't..." His voice broke, and he stopped. Then he took a new breath and tried again. "When you said no, and I thought I'd lost you both..." His chest heaved.

"I will marry you, Bennett Cobb. I will."

"Yeah?"

"Yeah." She smiled. It was so easy now. Of course they belonged together forever. "We'll be a family, and you'll be Lovie's daddy. Her real dad, the one who gets to see her grow up and pay her parking tickets and lead her down the aisle at her wedding."

Bennett stirred. "Do you want to see the ring?"

Sisley laughed. Before, her soul spilled over in tears. Now it was laughter. What would it be once they were married? How radiantly happy could one person be before they burst into sunshine and bubbles? "Yes! Show me."

Bennett opened the box. Sisley's mouth fell open, and now it was him who laughed. "You like it?"

"It's perfect!"

He pulled the pear-shaped solitaire from the cushion. "Not imperfect like me?"

She held out her hand and smiled. "I never said you were, Bennett. To me, you're perfect too."

"I love you, Sisley." He kissed her hand with the ring on it, and then he kissed her on the lips until she thought her heart would fly from her chest and her knees would buckle, and she had to break away to gasp for air.

"I love you too, Bennett," she replied when she could, and then he led her out of the tunnel and into the light of a bright, sunny future.

CHAPTER 24

Mela cleared her throat. Sisley and Bennett were beaming at her from the living room couch, their faces as happy as the bright morning light that cheerfully danced over the coffee cups and plates with leftover breakfast rolls on them.

"Of *course* you have my blessing." She turned to her friend and laughed when she saw her face. "I'm sure Amelie will say the same once she can speak again."

Amelie's tissue was pressed to her mouth, but she didn't need words to nod, so she did.

"Thank you, Mother," Bennett said. "Thank you, Mela."

"It means a lot to us." Sisley cleared her throat, clearly torn between crying and laughing herself.

"Tell us one more time how it happened," Amelie demanded. The tissue moved from lips to eyes and back.

Sisley sweetly obliged, repeating the harrowing hunt in the tunnels of Beach Cove and the moment they found each other.

"Good! But you are never to go back into that basement again!" Amelie shook her head. That part of the story only now registered with her. Both of them had spotted the diamond on Sisley's finger the moment she walked into the door, but they'd pinched their lips shut and not asked until she and Bennett made the announcement.

Mela still couldn't believe it had happened. After all her reservations about relationships, Sisley's smile suddenly had the wattage of a super trooper.

"We'll be in-laws, Amelie. How about that?"

Tissue and hands dropped into her friend's lap. "Finally! Heaven knows it took them long enough."

"All good things take time," Mela said sagely. In fact, the kids had found each other in record time. But Amelie had waited for years for Bennett to marry.

"I should have realized that I loved you right away," Sisley admitted and spread her fingers to let the new rock flash in the light. "But I thought I needed to be on my own."

"You also thought I was dating someone else," Bennett teased and pulled her to him.

"You did look pretty cozy with Sophia when I saw you in the café." Sisley giggled and struggled free. "Your faces were definitely in the kissing zone."

"Only because we exchanged classified information." Bennett kissed the top of Sisley's head. "We didn't want the fishermen's wives at the next table to go looking for our perp. They caught a few words in the beginning and were all ears after that. I think one of them took notes on her phone." He shook his head.

"Well, from now on, I should be the only woman you exchange classified information with."

He grinned. "Got it."

"Good." Sisley gave him a peck on the cheek, and then she got up and went into the kitchen to clang around with the coffee maker.

Amelie leaned forward. "Have you shown her the house?"

Bennett nodded. "When I got back from Beach Cove last night." His eyes shifted as if he didn't care to talk about last night with Amelie—or Mela, for that matter.

Mela swallowed a smile.

"And? What did she think?" Amelie held her breath with anticipation.

"She cried." Bennett sighed dramatically.

"Why?" Amelie pulled her chin back. "Don't you like the house?"

"I *love* it." Sisley came back into the room with the refilled coffee carafe, Julie's long skirt swinging. Again, Sisley looked so much like her grandmother.

Julie should have had a story like this too—a marriage proposal, a diamond, a husband free to worship the ground she walked on.

Sisley cleared her throat as if the tears threatened to rise again. "Everything was so perfect. I needed a moment to process it."

"What house?" Mela looked around. "What house, Sisley?"

"Strap yourself in, Mom. We're going to be neighbors." Sisley put the coffee on the table and kissed Mela's cheek. "Bennett bought the house on the other side of the lilac hedge."

Mela's eyes widened. Sisley would be next door? "Amelie! Did you know about this? Why didn't you tell me? I can't believe you!"

"Well, she didn't buy the house. I did." Bennett sounded concerned. "I told her not to say anything to anybody."

"Still, Amelie! I would've..." Mela pressed a hand to her forehead. She wasn't sure if she felt dizzy or surprised or happy or betrayed. It was a lot for one morning.

Amelie ducked her head guiltily. "I wasn't sure how it all would play out, Mela. I figured it was better to let Bennett be the one to spread the good news. You know...once he *had* good news."

Mela jumped up. "I was worried Sisley and Lovie would live across town or move away altogether now that Kimmie and Travis—but now you will be right next door!"

"I thought you would like that." Bennett sounded relieved.

Sunny came back from a walk. "What's going in here?"

Mela turned to her. "You had better sit down."They brought her up to speed, and once she had gotten over the surprise and past the hugs and kisses, Sunny fell back into her armchair. "Mela, you and both your daughters are neighbors now," she marveled. "Lovie can come and go between houses without even having to step on the sidewalk."

Bennett nodded. "I already have a spot picked out where we can cut the path."

Sisley rubbed her hands over her face. "I can't be this happy," she said weakly. "It's too much."

Bennett didn't say anything, but he smiled and took her hand. If Mela could have kissed him on the cheek without getting in the way of Sisley's adoring gaze, she would have. Sisley would be so happy with him. So happy.

Amelie elbowed her lightly in support, and Mela swallowed the threatening tears of joy.

"So when is the wedding?" Sunny asked. "Soon?"

"We'd like a beach wedding," Sisley said. "So we're looking at June or even July. It's going to be too cold before that."

"Oh." Amelie looked crestfallen but rallied quickly. "Next summer. That sounds lovely. But, um..."

"But we're moving in together now," Bennett announced firmly. "I'm not waiting for the weather."

Sisley nodded her agreement.

Mela smiled at her daughter. "It's good to see you so... so.... Oh. After the way Lars treated you... It's good to see you so...*engaged*."

Everyone started to laugh, and even Mela had to hiccup a laugh. Then she took a deep breath, crumpled the tissue into a ball, and stood. "Congratulations, my dears. I couldn't be more delighted. I hear cars coming up the street, and Peter and Charlie will be here in a moment. Amelie and Sunny, can you help me clear the breakfast and bring out the pie?"

Breakfast had been some time ago—the kids had asked to see her and Amelie before everyone else joined them. Now the morning was going on noon, and Sunny had baked apple pie for a pre-lunch treat.

"Yes!" Sunny jumped up. "Let's set the patio table. It's nice and sunny."

Bennett rose too. "Mela, do you have a moment for me?"

Everybody looked up

"I just want to properly ask Mela's permission. I'm marrying the daughter of my mother's best friend. Any cut corners will be the dinner discussion of years to come." He smiled.

Amelie narrowed her eyes, but Mela nodded at her. "Sure," she said. "Come on, Bennett. Let's go out onto the patio for a moment."

"Thank you." Bennett exchanged a glance with Sisley that made Mela glad—at least he and her daughter had no secrets from each other. Sisley knew what he was going to say.

Bennett unlocked the sliding door and let her go first, then closed the door again. Down at the beach, the sea hummed its eternal melody. Mela inhaled the crisp fall and went to the low garden wall as if the rough field stones could ground her. "What can I do for you, Bennett?"

"About that beach yesterday," he started carefully.

"Yes. Finn's beach." Mela nodded. "Is that why you went there?"

"No. I didn't know he liked the beach until Sisley told me. I just followed the man I was looking for."

"So you spent your free day working," Mela observed. "I hope you don't plan on doing that once you're married." She tried to look stern.

He smiled. "Not if I can help it. Work is not as fun as I make it seem."

Mela smiled back. "What about that beach?"

"I saw my perp going down the bluff onto the beach and disappear from view, so I followed. I'm heavier than he is, so I broke the staircase along the way." He sighed. "When I did finally manage to get down, I'd lost him. I was searching for something to tell me where he'd gone."

"Like what?"

His left eyebrow lifted. "A gum wrapper. Tracks... I don't know. Just something to indicate where he went. I had no idea the tide would completely cover the beach. Nor, to be frank, did I realize the tide was coming in."

"Always keep one eye on the sea," Mela couldn't help repeating what Julie had drilled into her. "We don't want you washed away."

"Believe me, I learned that lesson yesterday. I was deep in the cave when it started to fill. I'd only spotted the tunnel above the rock ledge because I was searching for something like that since my guy had simply disappeared. Anyway, the water rushed in, and I was scrabbling around in half a panic trying to get back to the tunnel..." He stopped himself. "All right, in a full panic." He showed his fingers, and Mela saw they'd been scraped raw.

Mela frowned. "That must've been terrifying."

"There was a rope ladder to get in and out of the tunnel, but I didn't find it until later. The perp had pulled it up once he'd gotten up there. My only chance was to stack up rocks high enough to pull myself up. I dislodged some big ones, and when I kicked loose the last one, there was something wedged under it."

"What?" The smile on Mela's lips had faded away, and she'd wrapped her arms around herself. Bennett wasn't out here to ask her permission. He was out here to give her a moment before she had to face the others. "Bennett. What did you find?"

He pushed his hand into the pocket of his sports coat to pull something out, then opened his fist. "This."

On his palm lay a delicate ring of tarnished gold. In the clasp of prongs shimmered three cobalt lapis lazuli stones, as star-speckled as the night.

CHAPTER 25

"Mela?" The detective climbed up the buff. She took off her knit cap and wiped her forehead, glancing at the glistening sea.

Mela stood up. It was sunny but cold; luckily, she'd brought a shawl. She pulled it closer around her. "Yes, Sophia?"

"They found wood that could well be from a wrecked boat." Sophia huffed, still catching her breath from the steep climb. "We're collecting what we can."

"Is there any paint left?"

"It might've been turquoise. Sound familiar?"

Mela nodded. "I do remember a turquoise stripe running along the hull. Sunny's trying to find the one photo she has of the boat." She took a breath to steady herself. "Did you find anything else?"

Sophia shook her head. "Not yet. We'll have to see what the dive team finds."

Martin, Sunny, Amelie, and the Townson brothers stepped closer, forming a circle of friends and family around Mela. A little farther off in another small group stood Sam and her husband David, Maisie and Vince,

Ellie on the arm of a burly fisherman whose name was Gordon, and Cate and her husband, Calvin. Sisley, Morris, Kimmie, and Johanna drifted between groups like the intersection of a Venn diagram.

Martin cleared his throat. He was leaning heavily on his cane, and Sunny supported his free arm. He looked exhausted. "How long will it take for the dive team to check?"

"I'll ask them when they come up," Sophia promised. "It depends on visibility and things like that."

"Why were they here?" Mela turned to Martin. She was still in a haze of disbelief. For most of her life, she'd been hoping to find her mother. Now that they seemed closer, everything seemed flipped upside down. She wasn't even sure anymore that she wanted to know what exactly had happened.

"I'd better go back down and help search," Sophia said. "Sorry I don't have better news."

"Better news," Mela murmured. "I'm not sure that exists."

"I'm not sure there's good news to be had here either," Martin said after Sophia was gone.

"Maybe it'll be better than not knowing," Charlie pulled Amelie closer to him. "It must be terribly draining to always wonder what happened."

"It wears you down, but you also still have hope," Martin replied. "If they find the kids, there's no more hope." He pressed his stick into the ground and sighed. "And yet—I want to know. I want to know before I die myself."

Mela nodded. "Me too. In the end, it might feel like you're closer to them when you know."

Ellie's friend Gordon, the burly fisherman, split from his group and joined theirs. "I remember hearing about Julie and Finn in the news back then," he said. "We fishermen saved more than one tourist from this beach. But we never thought these two might be in Beach Cove. The currents should have carried them in the opposite direction. That's where they searched."

Martin nodded. "You and your dad did all you could back then, Gordon. Finn must've tried to bring the boat here. Maybe he wanted to show Julie his favorite beach. But Finn didn't know the cove. Not as a sailor."

Gordon nodded. "The cove looks harmless enough, but it's dangerous if you don't know what you're doing. There's a ring of rocks where the cliffs form the gate that rips hulls like they're made of paper. Even if you have a nautical chart to steer you, navigating them is a dance with a drunken lover. My family has fished here before there was a proper town, and the steps of that dance are in our blood. Finn was a teacher, not a sailor, and I can't find that he ever talked to one of my men about crossing the cove. If he tried to get to this beach on his own, he wouldn't have had a chance."

Martin lifted his chin as he squinted over the treacherous water to where the cliffs guarded the cove. Then he looked at Mela. "I'm sorry. I wish my son had known better than to try the cove. If he'd asked me, I'd have checked with Gordon. But he didn't ask because I wasn't as good a father to him as I should've been. Maybe you can find it in you to forgive him."

A small, sad smile tugged on the corner of her mouth. "I'm not angry, Martin. They both were my parents, and I know deep in my heart that they did the best they could. Would I be alive if it wasn't for them stumbling along, trying to find a way?" She shook her head. "We all do it, don't we? Making it up as we go along. Kids, marriages, cliffs... It doesn't always work out the way we hope." She exhaled. "I just hope it didn't take long." She shuddered.

"If they ran the cliff, it was quick," Gordon promised. "I saw it happen before we put out the buoys."

"Hmm." Mela didn't want to picture it.

"I'm sorry, Mela." Peter put an arm around her, but for once, it didn't make her feel safe. She opened her hand and looked at the lapis lazuli ring. She'd forgotten that it had three stones, as flecked with gold as the night sky; and yet, now that she saw it again, she remembered each individual stone. As if a rock had not only been turned in the cave unearthing the ring but also in her memory to reveal lost images.

She swallowed and closed her hand over the ring again, and then she shrugged free and walked to the end of the bluff.

They'd been asked to wait up here so they would be safe and not accidentally destroy evidence. Since the man Bennett and Sophia had been chasing had lived in the tunnels, officers were searching for more than just evidence for her parents' shipwreck.

Mela watched for a while, listening for the calls of the searchers and the rushing of the tide as it drew back, leaving behind a perfect half moon of sand as white and fine as sugar. When she next looked up, she saw Sisley at a little distance. Her daughter, too, was standing at the edge of the bluff as she watched Bennett, her fiancé and best friend, comb the beach. Her long blond hair was fluttering in the breeze, its cheerful dance mirrored by the long, loose skirt of Julie's dress fanning behind her.

Gordon was right.

It was exactly how everyone had said it must have happened all along; Julie and Finn lost control of the ship and drowned in each other's arms. Tears filled Mela's eyes, blurring the picture of Sisley, of Julie, looking out over the cove. Her last thought must've been of the daughter she was leaving to fend for herself.

"Mom?" Sisley suddenly held her hand. "Are you all right?"

Mela blinked her eyes clear. "I'm so afraid she suffered," she whispered. "I can deal with the fact that she died...but not like this. Not drowning for nothing."

"It wasn't for nothing, Mom," Sisley murmured. "They had fun, and then they had an accident. It happens."

"She must've been so desperate knowing I'd be all alone."

"You had it worse, Mom. What you went through was *worse*." Sisley hugged her.

Mela held on to her daughter. "I didn't die. I went on my merry way."

"She only died for a moment," Sisley said softly. "You were in foster care for the rest of your childhood."

Mela broke their hug. "What a strange thing to say."

Sisley's lips moved as if she was trying to form the right words. "Sometimes," she said finally, "it's like I can hear her talk."

Mela stared at her. Already, the resemblance was uncanny. "You hear Julie's voice in your head?"

Sisley shook her blond hair. "More like a murmur in the wind or a whisper in the grass. Sometimes, it's just a feeling." She smiled, embarrassed. "Pardon the purple prose. Do you think I'm crazy?"

Mela took her hand. "I don't know, sweetheart. Are you?"

"No." Sisley's smile deepened. "At least I don't feel crazy. Sam says it's just my intuition. She says she hears feelings too."

Mela glanced at the tall, pale woman. There was nothing purple about her. In fact, she seemed more practical than many others. Sam was standing with her feet planted firmly apart, arms crossed, talking calmly with her friends.

Mela returned her attention to her daughter. "What does she say? Not Sam. Julie."

"Different things at different times. But I rarely hear her." Sisley hesitated. "But just now, while I was watching them search down there... I felt like she hit her head and lost consciousness."

"She said that?"

"No, it was only a feeling. Like *I* hit my head. Like I was hit by lightning. But only for a second. Then it was like everything softened and lit up in white light."

"While you were standing by the edge of the bluff? That sounds dangerous, Sisley. Maybe you should see someone after all."

"I'm fine. Just... I know it was Julie. I think she showed me what happened to her."

Mela shook her head. "Why?"

Sisley raised her eyebrows as if it was obvious. "So that I can tell you, Mom. Julie wants you to stop wondering and worrying. She wants you to stop searching. It's over now. Can't you feel it too?"

Again tears rose to Mela's eyes. Whether Sisley was making up a story to make it better or not, no mother wanted her child forever wondering and worrying about her. Not for so long. Not for a lifetime. Mela wouldn't want her daughters to go through it even for a single day.

"Here." Mela opened her hand and showed Sisley the ring. "I want you to have it. You are so much like Julie. I shouldn't even be surprised she's talking to you."

Sisley picked up the ring and studied it. Then she handed it back. "This ring is for you, Mom. I'm sure your mother wanted *you* to have it. Put it on."

"I...can't." It would forever remind Mela of what had happened.

"Remember *her*, not what happened. That was only a moment, over in a flash. She wants to be with you even more than she wants to be with me," Sisley murmured.

"Maybe if you listen and aren't so scared of what you'll hear, you will feel her too."

Mela didn't know what to think. She'd never had a conversation like this with anyone, let alone Sisley. She slipped the ring on her finger. "It fits perfectly."

"Of course it does." Sisley hugged Mela, and then she walked away, back to the group of Beach Covians who was now having a heated discussion over something.

"What was that about?" Peter stepped beside Mela. "Are you okay?"

"I am," Mela replied. "Sisley told me to wear the ring." She held up her hand. "And, um...she said Julie didn't suffer. She hit her head, and it was over."

"How would she know that?" Peter lifted Mela's hand to admire the ring. "It's beautiful."

"She said she just does." Mela didn't think she should repeat that Sisley heard the wind murmur and the grass whisper.

Peter kissed the tips of Mela's fingers before warming them between his own. "There's one in each family." He smiled. "My mother was like that, Mela."

"Did you believe her?"

He shrugged. "I wanted to. I think that meant more to her than whether or not I did."

"Honestly, I'd prefer my dead mother doesn't communicate with my daughters." Mela shook her head, the three stones smooth under her fingertips. "So...Julie, Mom, if you can hear me—stop it. Talk to me, if you have something to say."

For a moment, the breeze rose into laughter and the waves rushed to write words in the water. But Mela couldn't understand them, and when the others joined her as if they had suddenly been summoned, she had to pay attention to the living not the dead, though love bound them together forever.

Read the next and last book in the Bay Harbor series! *Seaside Tides* continues the stories of families and friends as they tackle old secrets and new beginnings with humor, heart, and hope.

Beach Cove Series

Return with Maisie to charming Beach Cove and meet a wonderful cast of friends, families, and unique characters. The beaches are warm and inviting, the sea bluer than it has any right to be, and the small town is brimming with secrets. Maisie and her friends take turns helping each other through emotional trials, bittersweet mysteries, and mistakes of the heart. For the free prequel to the series, subscribe to Nellie's newsletter on her Facebook page or at https://BookHip.com/KMSQRTT

Bay Harbor Beach Series

Visit the seaside in the small town of Bay Harbor, meet new friends, and lose yourself in the riveting saga of strong women starting over. Walk quaint streets smelling of salt water taffy, browse cute stores for that elusive perfect swimsuit, and skip over the beach toward the sea because the sand is too hot – but most of all, find out how old friends and new neighbors help each other overcome everyday challenges and take second chances.

ABOUT THE AUTHOR

Nellie Brooks writes heartwarming women's fiction with relatable characters who face challenges ranging from bitter to sweet. After years of traveling the world and studying the behavior of animals (that appear in her stories), she turned to writing fiction. Her books are set in Maine, where Nellie likes to spend time on the beach with her family. Visit www.nelliebrooks.com to subscribe to her newsletter and find out more. You can also follow Nellie on Facebook and BookBub.

Made in the USA
Middletown, DE
09 October 2023